Too Many Clues

A Sebastian McCabe—Jeff Cody Mystery

Dan Andriacco

Paperback ISBN 978-1-78705-477-6
ePub ISBN 978-1-78705-478-3
PDF ISBN 978-1-78705-479-0

Published by MX Publishing
335 Princess Park Manor, Royal Drive,
London, N11 3GX
www.mxpublishing.com
Cover design by Brian Belanger

This book is dedicated to my friend

Felicia Carparelli

who shares a birthday with Sebastian McCabe

CONTENTS

Chapter One
Crisis Communications

When your job description includes the words "crisis communication," there are going to be times you wished you hadn't answered your smartphone. And when I saw that it was Maggie Barton calling me the day after Thanksgiving, I knew this was going to be one of those times.

"Cody's Carnival," I said by way of greeting. "This way to the sideshow."

The old gal giggled.

Such banter was normal between us, as readers of these chronicles will recall. Maggie had been reporting on St. Benignus University for the *Erin Observer & News-Ledger* my entire career as SBU's communications director, going back to its days as St. Benignus College. In fact, I'm pretty sure she pecked out her first stories on a manual typewriter. Her age is north of seventy-five and her hair looks like pink cotton candy.

"Hi, Jeff. How are you?"

"Blissfully ignorant up to now."

I'd taken a day away from the office to digest turkey and pumpkin pie, but there's no such thing as "off the clock" with a 24/7 job like mine.

Knowing that Maggie hadn't called to ask about my health, I frowned as I looked over at Lynda on the couch. She was nursing the boys at her womanly bosom, one on each tap, with their sister Donata paging through a picture book next to her. Lynda is an old-fashioned girl, and breastfeeding is so old it's new again. I felt warm all over watching her, despite the ominous phone call. Readers, meet Sam and Jake Cody, age fourteen months. Jake is the adventurous one, just like his namesake grandfather. We now have three children and a mini-van, though Lynda refused to part with her yellow Mustang.

Not a half-hour earlier, over our healthful breakfast of oatmeal with raisins and bananas, Lynda read me my daily horoscope from the *Observer*. This was a new practice acquired since she'd left the daily grind.

"Listen to this, darling: 'You'd be so bored if people always did as you preferred.'"

No, I wouldn't.

In that innocuous message, about as helpful as a fortune cookie, there wasn't the slightest clue that we stood at the precipice of a case that had the most gut-wrenching solution in Sebastian McCabe's entire amateur sleuthing career.

"What happened?" I asked Maggie.

"I'm calling about Warren Burch."

Oh, crap.

"What about him?" *As if I didn't know.*

"I thought he chose to retire as dean of the business school after the vote of no-confidence. That's the way it was presented at the time. But a source tells me that he was forced out after three women accused him of sexual harassment and an investigation verified their accounts. I understand he got paid to sit out the 2017–2018 academic year and then come back this year as a full professor teaching just two classes for the Financial Economics major at a nice salary. Is all that true?"

"I guess 'nice' is a matter of opinion, Maggie. It's not a very precise term."

To be precise, the weasel earns two and a half times what I do. Well, I wouldn't say "earns."

Lynda, who could hear both ends of the conversation, rolled her gold-flecked brown eyes at me. She does that a lot.

"Oh, come on," Maggie said. "Spill, Jeff."

When I write my magnum opus on public relations, I plan to devote a chapter on how to not stonewall the media. It just never works. The obfuscation itself becomes the story, and those stories don't die quickly. So, I had to answer Maggie—but carefully. The Warren Burch business was a tough one.

Burch had been dean of the Gulliver Mackie School of Business and Economics at SBU for just three years. In that short time, his dictatorial management style had the faculty from which he was promoted in an uproar. Lesley Saylor-Mackie, our executive vice president and provost, wanted to give him the boot after the second year. She hesitated, however, because Burch had been publicly critical of her husband for donating so much money to the school that they named it after him. She thought that removing Burch might seem like payback for the raspberries.

Then came a faculty vote of "no confidence" in his leadership and a series of accusations by female students. I originally thought they were all work-study students, but most of them were interns. What, you don't know the difference? Work-study students are in it for the money, meager though it is. They have a financial need. Interns, who may not even be paid, are on a career path.

"I would be careful about using the term 'sexual harassment,'" I advised Maggie.

"I'm told that the young women who filed complaints said he leered at them, made them bend over to pick up things, asked them to stand on a stool to adjust an air vent, and asked for dance lessons. Is that incorrect?"

Damn.

"No, it's not incorrect. Those were some of the allegations."

I could hear Maggie's computer keys clicking rapidly. "There were others, then? What else did he do?"

"I'm at home, Maggie. I don't have the details of all the accusations handy."

"But there was an investigation and a report of findings, wasn't there?"

"Yes. The dean of students and the director of employee relations wrote a report. They concluded that Dr. Burch violated the university's Values & Ethical Responsibility Policy by not respecting student employees in that he engaged in belittling and demeaning actions and statements."

In other words, he's a skank.

"That's not a direct quote," I clarified. "As I indicated, I don't have the report in front of me."

"But you're saying the allegations were verified by the investigation?"

"The investigators found them credible, although there wasn't enough evidence to say that Dr. Burch engaged in sexual misconduct. They also concluded that, in various ways, Dr. Burch fostered an unhealthy culture of fear, intimidation, and bullying among the faculty and staff of the business school." That *was* a direct quote, though I didn't say so. "The resolution of 'no confidence' approved by the business-school faculty said much the same."

"And that's why he resigned as dean?"

"His departure from that position was mutually agreed upon with senior administrators of the university as being in the best interests of St. Benignus." *Translation: We reached a quiet settlement.* "However, he still has much to offer as a valued member of the faculty." *A huge ego, for one thing.*

"Soft landing," Maggie muttered. "Could I have a copy of that report?"

"I'm sorry, but no. We are a private institution, as you well know, and I can't share that with you. It might contain information that would reveal the identity of the women involved."

She might have pointed out that Burch's name was being made public, so why not his accusers? And I would have volleyed back by pointing out that it wasn't the university's choice to make this public. But she didn't go there. That line of thought wouldn't have occurred to her.

"Why wasn't Burch terminated?"

"Terminated" always sounds like a mob hit to me. Maybe that's what Maggie had in mind.

"First of all, Dr. Burch is a tenured faculty member. His actions, while deplorable, were not illegal and did not rise to the level of warranting dismissal of a faculty member with tenure." Lynda glowered at me as I said this, and Donata pouted. They look a lot alike, what with the curly hair of a honey-blond hue. (Donata's hair started out a nice shade of Cody red, but changed its mind.) The boys just appeared contented and well fed. I turned my head so that I couldn't see my adoring family while I dealt with this ticklish work issue.

"Also, there is nothing in Dr. Burch's file to indicate any inappropriate behavior in the classroom or any other venue over his decades at SBU before he became dean. He had an excellent reputation as a demanding but brilliant teacher." *But he's still a skank.*

Maybe ascending to the ranks of administration as dean so late in his academic career had caused some formerly tight screws to go loose. Who knew?

"How much does he make as a full professor?"

"As a private institution, we don't reveal faculty salaries."

"But a lot?"

"Our salaries are competitive."

Though mine is giving Burch no competition at all.

"Gosh, Jeff, it does sound to me like this man is getting off awfully easy."

That's what Saylor-Mackie thought.

"On the contrary, Maggie. Look what happened: The university had several reports of highly inappropriate actions by the dean of one of our major schools. We investigated those accusations, verified them, and took action. Dr. Burch is no longer the dean."

"Why didn't you make this public before, all the events leading up to his resignation?"

"It's a personnel matter." The university also agreed not to make a public announcement of the reasons as part of our settlement with Burch, under which he agreed not to sue us to get his deanship back. But I didn't see any need to overburden Maggie with details like that. "Normally, we don't talk about personnel matters at all. Most private employers don't—or even public ones, for that matter. Since you had some information, though, I wanted to be sure you had it right." *I'm such a pal!*

"You could be even surer if you gave me a copy of the report."

"Nice try, Maggie."

We sparred a little more, but she didn't lay a glove on me.

"Don't be surprised if this shows up on the front page," she said at the end.

"Nothing surprises me anymore."

"Well, give my love to Lynda and the kids."

"Will do."

Lynda labored for almost fifteen years in the vineyards of the *Observer & News-Ledger* and its parent company, now known as Grier Newspaper Group. These days, though, her business card reads "Lynda Teal Cody, *Storyteller.*" That descriptor encompasses fiction, non-fiction, and podcasts. Lynda finished the first draft of her Kentucky family saga novel, *Bluegrass,* while on maternity leave and decided not to go back to the daily drudge. She was still polishing the manuscript, which included the addition of entire new chapters. I call her a recovering journalist, given that she's still close to her friends at the *Observer* and reads their output with great critical attention every morning. For instance, she shrieked the morning she read an obit in the print edition that began "A funeral Mass will be celebrated at xxx A.M. on xxxx xxxx . . ." Somebody forgot to fill in the x's.

"I love watching you work," she said after I extracted myself from Maggie.

That must have been irony. With her oval face and adorably crooked nose, honey-blond curls spilling over the generous curves on display in her form-fitting red turtleneck —where was I? Oh, yes. My beloved is much too lovely to be sarcastic, so it must have been irony.

"I was just trying to be transparent," I said.

"Well, it worked, darling—I could see right through you."

Her fingernails were painted like candy corn, matching her earrings. At least they weren't approximately 110 percent sugar, like the real thing.

"Burch gives me the willies, I must admit," I admitted.

"I was disappointed in Father Pirelli and Saylor-Mackie," Lynda said. The good father is our legendary president, but his executive vice president and provost calls most of the shots day-to-day. "I can't believe they didn't fire that creep. I know there wasn't any love lost between him and Lesley."

The Burch brouhaha wasn't a topic of conversation at Chez Cody the first time around because Lynda was still an agent of the Grier media empire at the time. So, I had to catch Lynda up a bit.

"Saylor-Mackie was advised to reach a settlement in order to avoid a lawsuit," I explained. The use of passive voice was deliberate, but it didn't save me.

"You mean advised by what's-her-name, SBU's top legal eagle?"

"Kelly Richards. Ultimately, yes. But I said it first."

"What?"

I winced. *Is it cold in here or is it just you?*

"Fighting a lost cause is expensive, Lyn, both in money and in reputation. If Burch sued, which was about as certain as an amateur drinker's hangover on New Year's Day, we would have settled before it got to court anyway. It was a lot easier just to cut to the chase."

"Why would you settle? Why not litigate?"

"Because he would have won, and probably kept his job as dean while we paid his legal expenses. I read about cases like that all the time in *Higher Ed Insider*. Heck, there have been a slew of cases where students disciplined by their university as a result of sexual assault allegations sued the school for lack of due process and won."

"Couldn't the students that he harassed sue the university under Title IX for not giving Burch the boot instead of a cushy new job?"

Colorfully put. You should be a writer.

Title IX of the Education Amendments of 1972 is the federal civil rights law that prohibits discrimination on the basis of sex in the programs and activities of educational institutions. It's done wonders for women's sports, but also comes into play in issues of sexual harassment.

"All three of the accusers said they wanted Burch out of the dean's office," I said. "They got what they wanted. It ain't pretty, I know—like sausage being made, excuse the cliché. But we live in a fallen world."

My philosophical musings didn't go over too well. If Lynda had been her flirty Italian mother, who is even more beautiful but tempestuous of temperament, I might have been in real trouble. I could tell by the way she pressed her lips together. Then her eyes lit on Donata, who was busy doing whatever almost-three-year-olds do with paper and crayons.

"Would you want him anywhere near our daughter, or our nieces?"

Low blow! Donata was too young even for Burch. But the oldest of the McCabe girls, Rebecca, is nineteen—nineteen!—and a sophomore at SBU.

"I don't even want him near *me*, Lyn. Fortunately, I'm pretty sure he'll be long gone by the time Donata walks the hallowed halls of SBU."

I sure had that right.

Chapter Two
Bad News

"In the doghouse, eh Jefferson?" Sebastian McCabe said. He pointed to Maggie's story in the *Observer*, which lay face up on a Chez Cody family room chair.

Arf!

"Nonsense," I said. "Lynda knows that I have a job to do."

"Remarkable woman, old boy. I have always said so."

On that fall Saturday afternoon, the day after my call from Maggie Barton, that remarkable woman was at lunch with her best gal pal and taekwondo classmate, Sister Mary Margaret Malone (Sister Polly to most, Triple M to me). Mac, spouse to my sister Kate, was helping me babysit. Considering that he is upwards of a hundred pounds overweight, with gray creeping into his dark beard, watching him get on the floor was a treat.

"She's an extraordinary newswoman, too," I said proudly.

"How so?"

"Lynda still believes in what used to be called the American model of journalism. You don't know what that is? I'm not surprised. We don't see a lot of it anymore. It's the old idea of trying to be fair to both sides. Some would even say objective, but maybe that's too much to ask. Fairness isn't, though. And Lynda complained over breakfast this morning that Maggie's story on Warren Burch didn't cut it on that score."

"I did observe a certain lack of balance in the account when I read it this morning."

"That didn't take a detective."

Under the cringe-inducing headline **SBU DEAN OUT—SORT OF—AFTER COMPLAINTS FROM 3 WOMEN**, the *Observer* story began:

> A former dean at St. Benignus University is still on campus as a highly-paid full professor despite three credible accusations of inappropriate behavior toward female students working in his office.
>
> Warren Burch resigned as dean of the Gulliver Mackie School of Business and Economics near the end of the 2016-2017 school year after the university received allegations by three students that he engaged in such bizarre behavior as asking for dance lessons and requiring them to adjust an air vent, apparently so that he could look up their dresses.
>
> The matter was investigated by SBU's dean of students and its director of employee relations.
>
> "They concluded that he (Burch) violated the Values & Ethical Responsibility Policy," said T. Jefferson Cody, SBU director of communications. Cody conceded that the investigation found Burch to be "not respecting employees through belittling and demeaning actions and statements." Such conduct apparently extended to faculty of the business school, whose resolution of no confidence in him as dean immediately preceded his exit.
>
> But Cody defended the administration's decision to return Burch to the business school faculty, saying . . .

And so forth. The story went on for another fourteen paragraphs, with Maggie treating her readers to more examples of Burch's less-than-sterling behavior. "Burch could not be reached for comment" was buried about mid-story. The quotes attributed to me were reasonably accurate, at least in spirit, but the tone was slanted throughout. The story would have undergone some heavy editing back when Lynda had been Maggie's boss.

The only good news about the bad news is that it was overshadowed by even worse news—the continuing opioid crisis or epidemic, whichever you call it. Both words fit. The Burch story was relegated to the bottom of the front page, while the top was given over to a story about a big battle at City Hall over whether Erin's Finest should carry naloxone (brand name Narcan) to bring overdose victims back from the brink. Our good friend Oscar Hummel, the chief of police, and Reverend Fred Sutterlee, who was elected mayor of Erin as a write-in candidate the year before, both supported the practice. As did Dr. Arlene Eppensteiner, Sussex County coroner, whose morgue had hosted a surge in overdose victims in recent months. Well, years, really, thanks to the adulteration of drugs with fentanyl, a powerful synthetic opiate mostly shipped from China. But some council members demurred, arguing that cops could be attacked by people they were trying to save.

Johanna Rawls had been writing opioid stories in the *Observer* for at least three years. I'd read enough of them to know that a lot of addicts started out as people in pain, not thrill-seekers. She once reported an estimate that eighty percent of heroin users said they started by abusing prescription drugs. Some of them were older folks drawing Social Security. Tall Rawls even wrote one story about patients who were afraid that the backlash against prescription opioids would doom them to a life of agony—or suicide. This was a nationwide problem, and small-town

Ohio didn't get a pass. In fact, Ohio ranked second in the nation in overdose deaths in 2016, according to the Centers for Disease Control. But the crisis was above my pay grade —unlike the depredations of Warren Burch.

"I'm not looking forward to going back to work on Monday," I told Mac.

As the tenured Lorenzo Smythe Professor of English Literature and head of the tiny popular culture department at SBU, Mac doesn't have to worry about work. He has plenty of spare time to toss off mystery novels.

"Perhaps the Burch story will be short-lived," he ventured.

"From your lips to God's ears."

I knew that God hadn't been listening when Lesley Saylor-Mackie called me first thing Monday morning. My inestimable assistant, Annaliese "Popcorn" Pokorny, had just put a cup of low-test coffee in my hand when the phone rang.

"Yes, Provost?"

I can never bring myself to call that formidable woman by her first name, despite our great working relationship.

"Kelly wants to see both of us right away, Jeff."

No summons from a lawyer can be good, even when she works for you.

"What did I do now?" I asked.

"I'm sure she'll tell us," Saylor-Mackie said wryly. "Be in my office in ten minutes."

That gave me plenty of time to finish drinking my defanged java. The Office of Communications (housing Popcorn, me, and the occasional work-study student) was only a floor below Father Joe and Saylor-Mackie in the Gamble Building. The latter had persuaded the president to move his offices from 1960s-era Carey Hall near to hers in the iconic edifice shortly after her promotion to executive vice president and provost. I'd needed no persuading to

depart Carey for the same greener pastures. The impressive
Georgian structure of the Gamble Building with its columns
dominates the older part of campus. The name comes from
Erin banker Josiah Gamble's great-grandfather, who funded
it decades before naming rights had a name.

"So how was Thanksgiving?" Popcorn asked, casually
nursing her own mud in the chair across from me as I
chugged.

"Oh, the usual. Mac cooked the bird and performed
other magic tricks. His parental units are in town for the
weekend. Mine Skyped in from Virginia. Lynda's mom sent
the kids an autographed picture of herself not looking
grandmotherly, and her dad called. How was your Turkey
Day with Oscar?"

Not quite five-foot-tall, a dyed blonde widow with
grandchildren, my assistant is the Chief's only squeeze. If he
squeezed any harder, she'd be a tube of toothpaste.

"Quite intimate," she reported.

"Okay, that's all I need to know!"

In her mid-fifties, Popcorn still reads those steamy
romance novels by the pseudonymous Rosamund DeLacy.
(*Love's Wild Desire* was the latest. How does that woman still
have time to write books?)

"It was just Oscar and me and his mother."

"Oh."

I made it to Saylor-Mackie's spacious walnut-and-
hardwood floor digs with two minutes to spare and walked
right in (the door is always open for me), but I was still the
last one to the party. The Provost and Kelly Jane Richards,
looking serious, sat in stuffed chairs around a small round
table to one side of the ginormous desk Saylor-Mackie
inherited from her predecessor. Saylor-Mackie's main
addition to the décor was a painting of William Howard Taft,
the subject of her award-winning biography.

"Come in," Saylor-Mackie invited, just as my butt
occupied the third chair. A former almost two-term mayor of

Erin, Dr. Lesley Saylor-Mackie is a terminally stately and commanding presence in impeccable dress (although not always the business suits she used to favor) and sandy-gray hair. Her sixtieth birthday is in the rear-view mirror, but not too far.

"Thanks," I said. "What's up?"

I aimed the question at the barrister, a fortyish, plus-size woman with a pretty face, wide brown eyes, and a distracting streak of white hair in an otherwise-black mane. Today she wore a tweed skirt, cream blouse, chunky silver jewelry, and rings on almost every finger. A pair of tortoise shell glasses rested on her head.

"Deep guano, Jeff. You got us in it."

I've always admired Kelly's unlawyerly ability to speak English.

"Maggie's story," I deduced. "What did I do wrong?"

She crossed her admirable legs, pulled her glasses down on her nose, and began reading from a document in the voice one uses when quoting. "'Neither party shall make any statements to third parties which are disparaging, derogatory or negative about one another.' That's what's known as a non-disparagement clause, remember? You've been involved with similar clauses in the past. In this case, that particular wording is part of the settlement I signed on behalf of the university so that we could get Burch out of the dean's chair without getting sued."

She should have used an Oxford comma after the word "derogatory" in that clause, but I didn't think this was the time to bring that up.

"I wasn't being disparaging," I pointed out. "I was being accurate."

"In this situation, Jeff, the truth is not a complete defense, as it is in libel cases. Evan Farleigh called me on my mobile over the weekend. He's pissed."

"Okay, that's *what* he is, but who is he?"

"Burch's lawyer," Saylor-Mackie said, keeping her hand in.

"Oh, yeah. Of Farleigh & Farleigh, on Main Street. Now I remember. Well, I see the problem and I'm sorry." I meant it. I mentally kicked myself in the mental posterior.

"You were trying to be transparent, and I appreciate that," Saylor-Mackie said. See why I love her? "What's Mr. Farleigh threatening, Kelly?"

"No specific threat. He just reminded me that the agreement is binding on both parties. He's going to write me a letter to that effect and I'm going to write him back an apology and a promise that we will never do it again. And then you will never do it again. Right, Jeff?"

"What if I get asked about my quotes in the *Observer* story?"

"You can't unbreak an egg, but don't say anything more."

"And that's it?"

"That's it. If we don't step in it again, it ends there. I know Evan very well. We were law school classmates at Chase. I'm quite certain that most of his outrage was manufactured so that he could truthfully tell his client he reamed me good." She smiled.

"As a historian, it's my instinct to take the long view," Saylor-Mackie said, "so I'm not as worried as I assume Jeff is about the story. But I do wonder who tipped Ms. Barton about the accusations."

"Mac and I chewed that over a bit the other day," I said. "He pointed out that Maggie knew the number of accusers. An accuser herself wouldn't necessarily know that. So, it sounds like somebody inside the administration with access to the report on Burch tipped her."

"Can we find out who?"

I shook my head. "I don't know how. Not from Maggie, for sure. You couldn't pry that information out of her cold, dead hand."

"I hope you called and expressed our displeasure with the story," Kelly said.

Self-control kept me from laughing. "It's not her job to please us. Her job is to get the facts straight. She did that. It could have been fairer—I don't like the tone at all. But tone is subjective. I once complained about the tone of a story and the reporter responded by delving back into the topic and wrote a new epic that was worse than the first." I shook my head. "I think it's best to let this sleeping dog lie."

If only Maggie had thought so! She got in a few more licks in Tuesday's *Observer* with a follow-up story quoting shocked students and the usual activists. The general mood of the piece was "off with his head." Old friend of mine that Maggie was, in a Stockholm Syndrome kind of way, that really rankled.

Lynda bemoaned the continued lack of balance, although an observer might argue that I added to that problem by declining further comment (as ordered). Evan Farleigh did get to defend Burch with a short quote two-thirds of the way through the story: "Dr. Burch acknowledges using poor judgement in some of his actions while dean of the Gulliver Mackie School of Business and Economics. Administration is not his métier. He is excited to be back to teaching, which is his first love and a profession at which he excels." (In academia, gracefully canned administrators always go back to teaching, which is invariably described as their first love.)

Other Ohio media, including our own student newspaper, the *Spectator*, hopped on board in due course. And then there was social media. Twitter and Facebook blew up with righteous indignation, some well-informed and most not. "*Do better SBU*," tweeted a student named Dale Curtis in one of the milder posts. "*Don't let him teach us.*"

Surprisingly, Burch had a defender in the person of an SBU student named Jason Danvers. He wrote an op-ed piece in the *Spectator* under the headline STAY CALM AND

CANCEL THE LYNCHING. The piece was overwritten and given to glittering generalities, like most undergraduate work—and all too much professional work these days, for that matter. "Dr. Burch is one of the most distinguished professors on campus, as attested by his many awards and recognitions," Danvers averred. "To deprive St. Benignus of his talents because of actions that were injudicious at worst would be folly in the extreme."

A line in italics at the end of the piece identified the author as *a fourth-year Financial Economics major.*

"Well, there's a fellow with an opinion," I said to Popcorn. "See what you can find out about him."

"I'm on it, Boss."

She reported back before the end of the day that Jason Danvers was on a track to get both BS and MBA degrees in just five years. The program was a popular one in our part of the state because it was a relatively quick way to get a masters, cutting the cost and getting the student into the workforce faster.

"Grades not spectacular," Popcorn noted. This wasn't public information, but she has her ways. "Also—and maybe this explains his interest—Warren Burch is Danvers's faculty advisor and one of his instructors. The course is 'International Economics and Finance.'"

"Well, there you are. He's sucking up to the old goat in full view of the *Spectator* readership. Thanks."

I picked up the phone and called Hadley Reams, the editor of the *Spectator*. I had that job myself when I was a student at St. Benignus College, as it was called in those long-ago days. Hadley should have graduated a year and a half earlier, but he took a gap year in addition to changing his major from political science to journalism.

"What's this Jason Danvers like?" I asked.

"Not as smart as he thinks he is. But he comes from a family successful in business, so I guess he'll do okay in Mackie. His father is an award-winning architect in Chicago and his mother is the Chief Financial Officer of a department store chain, but they're divorced."

"How come you turned over a good chunk of a page to him?"

"Controversy sells newspapers," Hadley said.

"The *Spectator* is free."

"That was a figure of speech."

After a little more give and take about this and that, I hung up thinking that—with any luck—I'd never hear of Danvers again. Such luck was to elude me, however.

After adding Danvers to my Twitter feed just to keep an eye on him, I went back to working on the next edition of *Ben*, our alumni magazine.

A few days later, on the last day of November, I was rushing out of the Gamble Building at the end of the day. Frolic was on my mind as I looked forward to celebrating Lynda's thirty-seventh birthday the next day at pricey-but-worth-it Ricoletti's Ristorante. The nieces were lined up to babysit and all systems were "go." But then my Friday took a bad turn as I almost bumped into the very person who had dominated most of my work-related thoughts for a week—Warren Burch.

"Cody!" he exclaimed.

"Guilty," I admitted.

By the luck of the draw, this was the first time I'd seen him in weeks. From being up-close and personal with his CV, I knew that Burch was sixty-seven years old. He didn't look it, despite a head that was totally innocent of hair. He somehow looked virile, like maybe he pumped iron. If I were casting a Superman movie, he would have made a great Lex Luthor.

"What the hell were you thinking of, talking to that reporter?" he demanded in a loud voice, oblivious to gawking passersby on the campus sidewalk. He wore a scarf, but no hat against the cold.

"I was thinking of doing my job, Warren." *Him* I had no problem addressing by his first name—except for the temptation to call him by a name I wouldn't use in front of my children.

"How dare you talk to me like that! I've given more than four decades of my life to this institution. I worked harder than anybody on the faculty. That's why they hated me, forced me out."

A vein pulsed in his neck. I felt myself getting warm, despite the November chill. Figuring that the non-disparagement clause likely applied to campus pathways as well as the printed page and the World Wide Web, I silently counted to five in German to cool down. *Ein, zwei, drei* . . . It's the only German I know.

"I'm sure that's true, Warren," I said finally in what I hoped was a placating tone. "I was only—"

"We have a deal. If you break it, so can I. And you'll be damned sorry if I do—you and everybody up the food chain to Pirelli. Don't forget that."

"I've already been reminded—"

But I was talking to Burch's back.

Chapter Three
Bad Fall

"You've been tense lately," Lynda observed the following Monday morning after breakfast. At that hour of the day, her Lauren Bacall voice is at its throaty best. "You really need to relieve some of that nasty old stress, *tesoro mio.*"

Be still my beating heart. With our three delightful offspring in the arms of Morpheus, the prospect of being in the arms of my beloved set my pulse racing. A lot of my time with Lynda these days involved diapers and yawns. The evening before, for example, we both fell asleep in front of our newly installed, formerly-live Christmas tree. (My yearly plea to invest in a forever-tree made of real plastic has so far fallen on deaf, though cute, ears.)

I consulted my smartphone for the time, not wearing a watch ever since Mac stole mine right off my wrist in one of his stupid magic tricks. 7:45. I was due at work in fifteen minutes, and the Gamble Building is a ten-minute bike ride from home.

"I guess I could get to the office a little late," I said, as though making a concession.

"Not right now, silly. After work."

"Oh. Well, then, I'll rush right home."

She wrinkled her eyebrows in puzzlement. "Home? What are you talking about?"

Where else would we—

"What are *you* talking about?"

"The gym, of course. You haven't made it there in weeks and, I'm sorry, darling, but it shows." She poked my tummy tenderly. "You've picked up a pound or two, and not just since Thanksgiving."

That's a lie! In truth, I'd put on more like *seven* pounds since the end of summer. Either Lynda was being diplomatic, or the additional avoirdupois was spread so evenly over my six-one frame that it didn't show.

"You know how hard I've been working out and watching what I eat since the twins arrived," she said, "and it's paid off." She pointed at herself.

Taking this observation as an invitation to survey my wife's shapely shape, I did so. "It certainly has," I agreed with unfeigned enthusiasm. "How long do you think the kids will sleep?"

"Heavy traffic?" Popcorn asked as she handed me a cup of coffee.

"Not especially. I just left the house a little later this morning. You know how one thing leads to another."

The woman had children, after all.

"What are you smiling about?"

"Just in a good mood."

The day passed without any new crises as we worked on the alumni mag, a news release about the upcoming December graduation, the first draft of a speech for Father Pirelli, and an inquiry from a sports reporter in Lexington about the departure of our men's baseball coach for a job at Transylvania University. Warren Burch slipped off my radar, and I didn't miss him a bit. I even had a few spare moments to check out the progress of the Cody IRAs and the college savings plans for the kids, all of which are age-appropriately balanced between stock and bond index funds. The results put a smile on my face. The bull still roared that month.

At five o'clock, I picked up my gym bag and pedaled over to Nouveau Shape, the co-ed facility where Lynda and I worked out together back when we could do that in the mornings. SBU's new health club remains on the drawing boards, but Nouveau is real and near campus. For that reason, it attracts a lot of faculty and staff. Nevertheless, I was shocked to hear as I entered the men's locker room, "Ah, Jefferson, a beneficent Providence has brought us here at the same time. Who better to instruct me on the use of these torture devices?"

I must be dreaming.

But no! Sebastian McCabe stood before me, decked out in about an acre of gray sweat suit. He wasn't even wearing a bow tie. Until this moment I had never imagined him doing an exercise more strenuous than getting up and down from his computer as he wrote his latest Damon Devlin mystery novel, *Quicker Than the Eye.*

"Let me guess," I said. "Research?"

"Alas, no." He sounded mournful. "At your sister's insistence, I read a book about improving one's health. It included a self-assessment that led to a suggested course of action."

"And the book told you to join a gym?"

"Not exactly. It recommended that I get my affairs in order. Kate was quite upset. We reached a compromise. In exchange for a sincere effort to reduce my Body Mass Index, I will be permitted to smoke one cigar a day."

"How many do you figure to smoke without permission?"

"All too few," he said gloomily. "I am under the cruel oppression of smoke-free mandates both at home and at work."

"Life is tough, so suck it up. I accept the challenge of being your Vergil through this Inferno."

I changed my clothes, stowed my bag in a locker, and marched Mac into the weight room. There I nodded to a few of the regulars I hadn't seen in a while, equally balanced between men and women. I recognized a financial planner, a dentist, a retired IRS functionary, a grade-school teacher, an artist, and Sussex County's prosecuting attorney, Marvin

Slade. Over the years I've seen Slade in a towel more often than I've seen him in a suit. Despite my involvement in murderous shenanigans with Mac, we don't generally run in the same circles. He's always friendly to me when we do intersect, though. I've often wondered whether he realizes that Lynda and I do socialize with his ex-wife, defense attorney Erica Slade, with whom his relationship is raucous and bitter on a good day.

With nodding and inconsequential comments to these gym-mates accomplished, I introduced Mac to the equipment. Trendy name aside, Nouveau Shape offers the usual array of treadmills, stationary bikes, elliptical machines, free weights, Nautilus machines, slant boards, sauna, swimming pool, and whirlpool that you find at your health club, give or take a few wrinkles here and there. Not that you see a lot of wrinkles at Nouveau; it's largely a younger crowd, except for the former IRS gal.

"You might want to start with a few minutes on an elliptical machine," I advised my reluctant brother-in-law.

"What does it do?" His tone of voice suggested that he was afraid of the answer.

"It's easy." No need to tell him that some people don't find that to be the case. "It's just like walking, but not as hard on your knees. My doctor says it's better than a treadmill. I'll show you." I positioned myself on the machine immediately to the left of Marvin Slade and gestured to Mac to climb aboard the one on the other side of me.

"Now you just grip these handles and move your arms back and forth as you move your legs," I said.

Mac grunted as he slowly moved his massive bulk into position.

"Been reading your comments in the *Observer* on the Burch business," Slade told me from the other side of my machine.

This was a bit of a bolt from the blue.

"Sorry to hear that," I quipped.

"I wish I could get that bastard into court on a sex charge."

I knew better than to ask what was stopping him. That would have sounded like a dare from an SBU representative.

"May I ask what is stopping you?" Mac asked, butting into a conversation uninvited, just like a veteran health club habitué.

Marvin Slade is an average-sized guy with horn-rimmed glasses and dyed brown hair that he carefully combs to hide the bald patches. Self-doubt is not one of his burdens. And, like most prosecutors, he likes to think of himself as a hard-ass. "Marvin Slade—Soft on Crime!" would not be a winning message for a yard sign. Lately he'd been getting a lot of ink for successfully prosecuting manslaughter charges against defendants who supplied fatal doses of opioids to friends or customers. More power to him on that one, I say!

"Ohio Revised Code Section 2907.06 is stopping me," Slade spat. "It defines the crime of sexual imposition. Nobody has publicly accused Burch of that—yet. I have my hopes."

"You seem rather, let us say, *invested* in Professor Burch's depredations," Mac pointed out.

I looked at Mac and saw that he was looking at Slade. I looked at Slade and saw that he looked grim. "I seem to remember that you have daughters, Professor McCabe. I also have a daughter who . . . let's just say—"

What he would have just said I'll never know, although from what I do know I could give it a good guess. His response was cut short by a thud, a scream, and a hearty "Hell and damnation!"

Sebastian McCabe lay sprawled at the base of the elliptical machine, a look of excruciating pain on his hirsute face.

I disembarked and knelt next to him. "Are you all right? What happened?"

"Do I look all right, Jefferson? No, I am not all right, blast it! I fell off this bloody thing and my ankle hurts like the very devil. I very much fear that I have broken it. Health club! Bah!"

Chapter Four
In the Dead of Night

"That's awful!" Popcorn said when I told her the next morning. Like all the women in his life, she has an inexplicable soft spot for Sebastian McCabe.

"It certainly is." I oozed sympathy. "He's hobbling around on crutches and milking it for all it's worth. And the timing is terrible! If this had happened before the auditions for *A Christmas Carol*, he might have landed the role of Tiny Tim." SBU's theater department was about to premier a musical version of the Christmas classic at its recently acquired Davenport-Lattimore Bijou Theatre[1].

Popcorn disfavored my humorous sally with a look of disgust. "And the ankle was really broken?"

"No. As a doctor, Mac's a good mystery writer. It's 'only' a sprain, which I understand can be more painful than a break. Not being athletic like him, I've never had either."

I was spared a rejoinder by the ringing of my office phone. The call was coming from the President's Office. That wasn't unusual, so I had no premonition of the bomb he was about to drop on me.

"Jeff Cody," I answered by way of standard greeting.

"Father Joe here, Jeff. Could you stop by my office right away? I've made a decision you need to know about. Lesley's already here."

---

[1] For how the acquisition came about, see *Death Masque* (MX Publishing, 2018).

For him to demand a command appearance *was* unusual. SOP was an email asking me to "stop by at your convenience."

"I'll be there before you can hang up, Father."

That was a slight exaggeration. It took about a minute to climb up the flight of steps to his corner office on the fifth (and highest) floor of the Gamble Building, at the other end of the hall from Saylor-Mackie.

On the way I tried to figure out what was brewing. Maybe it had something to do with the upcoming capital campaign to fund major new construction on campus. Grant Kingsley, chairman of the board of trustees, was leading the charge. But any communications about that wouldn't prompt a call to be in Father Joe's office right away. What else could it be? A decision, he said. I couldn't think of anything that was awaiting a thumbs up or down from the corner office, so maybe it was a new initiative he was launching. Never a dull moment.

Reverend Joseph Pirelli—"Father Joe" to at least half of Erin—looked the same as always. Seated behind a desk much smaller than Saylor-Mackie's, with his cottony white hair and his age-defying lack of wrinkles, he seemed relaxed, rested, and ready for whatever was next. But the grim expression on his executive vice president and provost's face made me ask, "Who died?"

Father Joe chuckled. "Hardly that, Jeff. I've simply decided to resign for the good of the university."

"You can't do that!" my mouth said before consulting my brain.

"Oh, yes, I can. And I will."

"I've already tried to talk him out of it," Saylor-Mackie informed me, "but he's a stubborn old man."

"Old is right," he said. "I've exceeded the Biblical four-score-and-ten by a good margin, not that it matters. Age is merely chronological, I've always said."

This whole conversation seemed surreal, almost an out-of-body experience. Father Joe, like Maggie Barton, had been around forever. Or so it seemed to me. They were part of the fabric of local life long before I arrived in Erin. He was even older than she, at seventy-nine. This was like the sun and all the planets were suddenly out of alignment. Father Joe wasn't just a living legend who was my ultimate boss. He played with my kids and talked to Lynda in Italian. True, he had essentially been a figurehead since the hiring of Saylor-Mackie's predecessor, Ralph Pendergast, to do the heavy lifting. And we all knew that he had to retire someday—he'd been musing about it for years—but not this day. Why now? He had given me a clue, my shocked mind realized.

"What do you mean, 'for the good of the university'?" I asked.

"The sign on Harry Truman's desk said, 'The Buck Stops Here.' As president of the university, I'm responsible for the agreement that let Warren Burch remain on our faculty despite his despicable behavior toward young women in his office while he was dean."

"Blame me," Saylor-Mackie and I said at the same time. In other circumstances, that would have been comical.

"Jeff suggested the settlement and Kelly Richards agreed," Saylor-Mackie reminded him, "but I'm the one who talked you into going along."

"But I did go along. What kind of leader would I be if I didn't take responsibility for my mistake?"

"Whether it was a mistake is a matter for debate," I said. "The alternative, firing a man who had tenure before he became dean, is no walk in the park. That's why I suggested the settlement, to spare SBU a lawsuit, bad publicity, and a bigger settlement in the end. But in any case, you shouldn't be the scapegoat."

His remarkable blue eyes looked bemused. "That's a Biblical concept, you know—the goat cast into the desert to carry away the sins of the community. It first appears in

Leviticus. I've often thought of writing a book about the concept of the scapegoat throughout history and cultures. But in this case the term doesn't apply. I'm not taking the hit for anybody else. I should have overruled you two, and the lawyer as well, and insisted that Burch be separated from SBU. Let me be clear: I don't blame you for giving me the advice you thought best. I blame myself for taking it. I've made up my mind. I'm going to resign immediately, not wait until the end of the school year. This is a resignation, not a retirement. I want you to make that clear in the press release you write, Jeff."

This was said in his "tough father" voice, which he'd hardly ever used on me.

"The timing is not good," Saylor-Mackie tried. "You would leave us rudderless for the rest of the academic year." It was less than a week before exams, and nine days before the end of the fall term.

"Hardly rudderless, Lesley. I'm sure the board will appoint an interim president and immediately launch a search for my permanent replacement."

"How do you expect them to find a good candidate if the next president is going to be threatened with job insecurity in fifty years?" I cracked in a desperate effort to cheer myself up.

Saylor-Mackie shot me a "we are not amused" look, but Father Joe gave a wan smile.

"It's been a good run, my friends, and an extraordinarily long one. But there is a time for everything under the sun, as Ecclesiastes says, and my time as president is up. I'm sorry to go out like this, but so be it."

"I feel like an orphan," Saylor-Mackie said. Her eyes glistened.

"And I feel like a failed father." He cleared his throat. "I didn't just call you here to keep you in the loop. We have a bit of planning to do together."

We did it. Father Joe would inform each board member confidentially by the end of the day, and the public announcement would go out the next day. I already had the press release mostly written in my head by the time I left the presidential quarters.

"This is a dark day," Saylor-Mackie said back in her office. "I think I need a drink."

"Have one for me. I've got too much work to do."

"All right, I will."

"Do you keep an office bottle?"

"Several."

Who am I to judge?

Popcorn was waiting expectantly when I got back to my office.

"Big news, Boss?"

"You could say that."

I told her.

"But that's not right!" she burst out.

"No, it stinks. I'm going to be infuriated with Burch eventually for his role in this, but I don't have time for that now. You and I need to get cracking. Father Joe wants to make the announcement tomorrow."

"Is he holding a press conference?"

"He says not, but I'm going to talk him into it. If he's going to fall on his sword, he might as well bleed in public."

"Ouch."

"Don't mind me. I'm just in a sour mood. The real reason I want to get him in front of the media is to have him deny in person any speculation that he was forced out. The public and the alumni love him as much as we do. It would hurt the university if the directors were blamed for his exit.

"But, news conference or not, we have to write the release with some quotes from him which I'll invent, based on what I know he wants to say, and he'll approve. And we need a retrospective on 'The Father Pirelli Years' for the new issue of the alumni mag. We'll have to tear out something to make room for it. Talk about a rush job!"

"Hire Lynda." After a quick dive into her desk drawer, Popcorn handed me my wife's business card. "It says here '*Storyteller*,' and Father is a heck of a story."

"That's a great idea! Lynda's a fast writer and she already has a running start on the subject. I bet she'll say yes in a heartbeat—her first freelance job. Kate can watch the kids for a few afternoons while she works her word magic."

"But *Ben* is almost ready to go to press. What do we cut out at this late date?"

"Hold that feature on the assistant chief of campus police and about half the letters to the editor."

"It sounds like you want me to write a glowing life story, kind of like an obit," Lynda said when I'd outlined the task over dinner of white chicken chili for three and mother's milk for two.

"That's the general idea, but you also have to interview the great man himself."

"Sure. Not exactly a chore. He's such a sweetheart."

"Fortunately, nobody expects *Ben* to be objective. Think of your story as a love letter from the university."

"I think I've got it, Chief."

I almost choked on my Caffeine-Free Diet Coke. "Chief?"

"Don't get used to it. Now what are you looking so sober about?"

"I was just thinking of the irony: Father Joe, who's innocent of any wrong-doing, is ending his career over this flap while the real villain will be giving his end-of-term exam as usual on Monday."

But I was wrong about that. Cal Daley, SBU's Director of Public Safety, interrupted my well-earned sleep at 12:13 A.M. the next morning.

"Sorry to bother you, Jeff, but I knew you'd want to know."

"Know what?"

"Warren Burch is dead."

I tried to clear the cotton-candy out of my head. "I'm sorry to hear that, but why——"

"The night security officer found the body in his office. He was bludgeoned to death, his head beat in. I've already called Father Pirelli and Provost Saylor-Mackie. My people are on their way to the scene. I thought you might want to join them."

Chapter Five
Campus Security

When the kids let Lynda sleep, she sleeps. Being rather fond of having my body parts all in working order, I didn't wake her before I left the house at an hour that could only technically be considered morning. I had no similar hesitation about rousing Sebastian McCabe. In fact, I was a little disappointed that he answered on the second ring.

"McCabe here!"

"You sound disgustingly alert."

"I have been writing."

So that's how he does it!

I quickly filled him in on what little I knew, ending with Cal's invitation to show up at the crime scene. "Do you want to go with me?"

"Of course, old boy! There is, however, a bit of a challenge. Will my crutches fit in your Volkswagen?"

"They'd better. I'm not going to drive your boat." Mac's vehicle is a '59 Chevy the color and approximate size of a fire engine. Since it's one of the few places left where he is permitted to smoke his ghastly Antonio de la Cova cigars, it smells like an ashtray on wheels. My car, a 1998 New Beetle, soldiers on despite being on its last—though seldom-used—legs. It hit me hard earlier that fall when VW announced the demise of the nameplate. Call me sentimental.

I left Lynda a note, replete with hearts, apologies, and a sincere hope that I would be back before she woke up so that I could help with the morning trauma.

Since Mac's crutches were adjustable, I adjusted them to a size that would accommodate Toulouse-Lautrec (height four-foot-eight). That part was easy. Getting Mac into my car, on the other hand, was like a Laurel and Hardy movie best left undescribed.

On the short drive, the Cody memory banks rewound to the last murder on campus,[2] seven years earlier. Back then I was a bachelor with "it's complicated" for my "Relationship Status" on Facebook. Now I was the father of three, comfortably settled into middle age with the love of my life. My world is perfect, if you don't count the frequent forays into crisis communications and the occasional homicide.

Speaking of which, it was going to be a bit of a dance to come up with a press release that (a) emphasized SBU's commitment to a safe campus, and (b) said something positive about Warren Burch, while (c) not being too obvious that I was putting lipstick on a pig. And all of this on the morning of the same day Father Joe intended to resign over the Burch fiasco!

Concern about campus security was a particularly tough bullet to dodge, even though we hadn't had a murder in a literal dog's age. What we did have some time back was a series of dorm burglaries, which created a big scare about personal safety. The burglar, a criminal justice senior named Pierce Brooks, crawled into student rooms through an air duct at a time he knew the rooms would be empty. When a campus officer finally caught him, Brooks tried to escape. The officer tazed him and Brooks suffered a near-fatal heart attack. Although the officer was cleared of any wrongdoing, nobody was happy about how this played out (especially Brooks). That's why veteran cop Cal Daley was brought in over Ed Decker, the long-time campus police chief, as head of a new Department of Public Safety. Cal was tasked with

---

[2] See *Holmes Sweet Holmes* (MX Publishing, 2012).

creating a kinder, gentler, but also effective campus safety strategy. *Good luck, Cal.*

"What are you thinking, Jefferson?" Mac asked.

"I'm thinking I wish I were still in bed."

He seemed to find this insufficiently reflective. "Only that?"

"While I'm wishing, I also wish I lived in a world where the only murders you had to solve were on paper."

The big guy pondered. "Well, given that you do not live in such a world, Jefferson—nor has anyone since the days of Cain and Abel—I am pleased to do my small part to even the scales of justice."

That was Sebastian McCabe's idea of humility.

The Gulliver Mackie School of Business and Economics stands on the campus quadrangle, next to Chemistry and Biology. The brick federal-style building, with arched windows and a bell tower, dates to 1923 but got a new name when the business school was created with the help of that generous gift from Saylor-Mackie's husband. Three campus police vehicles and an EMS van were parked outside. Lights blazed inside, on the second floor. I showed my campus ID to an officer who looked about three days from retirement. Mac did likewise.

"Okay, you're expected," the officer said. He logged in our names, our positions with the university, and the time.

I felt a pang of conscience, but only a small one, when I saw Aurelia Banfield standing in the doorway of the Financial Economics rabbit warren with her boss, Ed Decker. My story about her for *Ben* was the one put on hold to make room for Lynda's Pirelli profile. And what a story! Ed's new assistant chief was an Ohio National Guard officer who lost a leg in Afghanistan and almost made it to the Olympics in 2016 as an archer. Mac, who met her first, described her as "Green Arrow without the angst." She'd returned from duty with the Guard's Counterdrug Task Force just before our interview. And just to put some icing on that cake, she's an SBU grad who majored in criminal justice as a non-traditional student.

Banfield saw us approach before Decker did. "Oh, look, Chief, the cavalry's here." How she managed to sound so cheerful at that ungodly hour was a mystery even Mac couldn't solve. She's thirtyish, muscular, and attractive. Doubtless roused from restful slumber just as I had been, she was clad in a sleeveless down jacket over jeans. Her angular face was framed in a blue knit cap which also covered her ears.

Decker grunted in response, at which he is well practiced. He's a big man—linebacker big, not too-many-doughnuts big—with black skin, a broad flat nose, and a thin mustache. He tossed his head toward the murder room. "The coroner said to send you right in."

"I am honored," Mac said.

"Not you, McCabe. Cody."

I live for moments like that. My life has so few of them.

It didn't surprise me that Dr. Arlene Eppensteiner, "Arly" on her campaign posters, was on hand even before the city cops. Since her election two years earlier, she'd made it a point to be on the scene of violent crimes—especially opioid-related deaths—although it wasn't part of the coroner's job description. She could have delegated, as most coroners do, but she was making a statement. Some people thought the statement was "Re-elect me!" For my money, though, she seemed sincere.

Mac and I went in, past an outer room with a small desk and a large photocopying machine which undoubtedly served several profs. Burch's office was one of several down a hallway. The full-professor-sized chamber was crowded with Campus Police, probably dusting for fingerprints and whatnot. An EMS type was talking to Dr. Eppensteiner, who wore a white lab coat over black slacks.

From where I stood, all I saw of the body was the feet sticking out. An unopened box of Chinese takeout lay nearby, as if he had dropped it. The rest of Burch's mortal remains was hidden by a wood desk, which was just fine with me given that whole "head beat in" thing. Mac slowly maneuvered himself for a closer look at the dear departed.

"Head wounds bleed a lot," he commented as he peered down.

Thanks for that image, Mac.

My active imagination filled out the picture with visions of Burch's bloody bald dome, so I looked around the room to distract myself.

Bizarrely, I noted an air vent right above the desk. Hadn't Burch required one of the women in his office to stand on a chair and adjust an air vent? But that had been in a different office, of course—the dean's office, from which he had been sent packing with a sweetheart deal that covered none of us with glory. What a tangle!

"Hello, Jeff."

"Arly."

I couldn't figure out whether it was the handshake of a politician or a doctor with which she greeted me, but it was firm and professional. We knew each other well enough to use first names—but who doesn't, these days?

"And what the hell happened to you, Mac?" she demanded to know.

Mac assumed an air of nonchalance, no easy task for a big man on crutches. "Good morning, Doctor. My attempt to improve my life expectancy through an exercise regimen was not a complete success."

She thought about smiling, then decided against it.

The coroner and I were of a similar age, namely mid-forties. But she's about a head shorter than me and her bobbed hair is jet black and curly, not red.

"You wanted to see me?" I said. It was a statement of fact, but I put a question mark at the end for politeness.

"Yes. Chief Decker and Assistant Chief Banfield have done a fine job of securing the crime scene. They also notified Chief Hummel of the Erin police, and I'm expecting his assistant chief to join us soon. But I wanted to touch base with you on the media relations aspect of this mess."

"Mess" was right. Not that the office was in disarray —at least, no more than any other professor's office, except for the Chinese takeout on the floor. Papers were scattered all over, sprinkled with dust and dirt, but Mac would probably call that *de rigueur*. His own hidey-hole over in Herbert Hall is a firetrap. No, the real mess here was that a professor had been murdered in his own office.

"I appreciate that," I told Dr. Eppensteiner. "Even though we're a private institution and the coroner's office is a public trust, let me assure you that SBU is as committed to transparency as you are. We want to be as open as possible in accommodating the public's right to know without impeding the investigation by law enforcement."

Damn, Cody, you're good!

"Well, we're on the same page, then. Especially the last part. I'm not here because I'm an insomniac, Jeff. I have the responsibility of investigating the cause of suspicious deaths in this county and I take that seriously. Whenever possible, I like to be the death investigator on the scene. In this case, it could hardly be anything other than homicide, but it's my job to make that call. As a side benefit, I sometimes talk to the ladies and gentlemen of the media when a case grabs their attention. I don't mind doing that."

Show me a politician who does.

"It's your show, of course," I assured Dr. Eppensteiner. "Believe me, I'll be happy to refer the press to you whenever possible."

"May I ask a question?" Mac asked.

Instead of pointing out that he just did, the coroner told him to go ahead.

"What was the murder weapon?"

She looked at me. "This is not for print, at least not yet. As in, don't tell your friends in the local media." Maybe she still smarted from that embarrassing mis-call during her third month in office. Her off-the-cuff reference to homicide at a death scene, duly reported by Johanna Rawls in the *Observer*, came back to bite her when the autopsy finding came out as accidental death by autoeroticism. "The blunt force trauma was inflicted with a heavy glass object, applied several times above the subject's right ear."

Mac tugged at the overgrown forest on his broad face. "What object, specifically?"

"Specifically, the Monsignor Francis B. Kennedy Award for Excellence in Teaching for 2005. We think it came from a credenza behind his desk."

"Ironic, isn't it?" Banfield observed.

"So, the killer picked up what was handy to use as a weapon," I said. "Doesn't sound like premeditation."

Nobody commented on my keen perception of the obvious.

In a detective story, this is where somebody would point out that the killer must have been right-handed, and somebody else would riposte that only ruled out the mere ten percent of the population that are lefties. But we skipped all that.

"Fingerprints?" Mac asked Decker.

"You gotta be kidding."

"Was anything stolen?"

"Who can tell?"

Decker had a point. None of us had ever been in the office before, so we wouldn't know if something was missing.

"Who found the body?" I asked.

Banfield took over. "The night officer, Jackson, discovered it on his rounds. He saw the victim alive earlier in the evening on his first time through the building. Apparently, from what Jackson said, it wasn't unusual for Burch to work late." *I'm surprised that Burch worked at all.* "Like all professors, he has a passkey. I figure he let his murderer in, by the way. Then, around eleven o'clock or so, during another pass through, Jackson heard the photocopy machine in operation and figured the professor was still at it. He knew Burch, so he decided to poke his head in and say 'hi' after he checked out the other floors. That was about twenty minutes later. He saw that Burch's office door was open, so he went in. Burch was there, all right, and apparently not long dead. Jackson called the Chief."

"This is nowhere near official," Dr. Eppensteiner said, "but warmth of the body and the thickness of the blood, or lack of it, is consistent with that narrative of events. That is, the timetable fits with the likely time of death, judging by external observation."

"I wonder what Professor Burch was copying?" Mac asked.

"What the hell difference does that make?" Decker snapped.

"Who can tell?" Mac threw his own words back at him. "I am also curious as to when Professor Burch went out for Chinese."

"Sometimes you think too much."

"Putting that aside, presumably Officer Jackson did not see the guilty party fleeing from the scene or someone would have mentioned that by now."

"That's right, Seb," Banfield said. *Seb?* "In fact, Jackson's adamant that he would have heard one of those heavy doors close from anywhere in the building as the killer left, except that he didn't."

"Covering his ass, maybe?" Decker said.

"Maybe, Chief. But it seems to me a killer familiar with the building could have played hide and seek for a while if he heard Jackson coming."

Decker shrugged his huge shoulders. "Anyway, I'm sure our bad boy will show up on the security video. We'll have that soon."

"Where is Jackson now?" I inquired. I knew him by sight, and he wasn't on the scene.

"I made him go to St. Hildegard Health. I'm pretty sure he was about to melt down. PTSD. He's a veteran, too."

"How about you?" Dr. Eppensteiner asked Banfield. "Are you okay?"

"I'm okay, thanks."

"The victim wasn't exactly your most popular faculty member, was he?" Dr. Eppensteiner asked. "I've been reading about him in the *Observer*."

You and too many others.

"We will not lack for suspects," Mac said. "At the very least it can be said with confidence that several young women will not greatly regret his departure from this earth."

Neither will Lesley Saylor-Mackie. I quickly unthought that, in case there were any mind-readers in the room.

"Just for the record, could a young woman have wielded that award with enough force to kill Professor Burch?" Banfield asked the coroner.

The good doctor didn't hesitate. "Of course. With enough adrenaline flowing, a young woman—or an old one, for that matter—could lift a car."

"I've seen it happen," came a voice from the doorway.

We all turned that way at the same time, like a bunch of synchronized swimmers. Lt. Col. L. Jack Gibbons, the deceptively average-looking assistant chief of the Erin police, looked apologetic. "Sorry I'm late. I guess this is my case."

"Not completely," Decker growled. Under Ohio law, campus police are sworn officers who carry guns and have the power to make arrests. This was a power that Ed Decker did not give up lightly. "We're going to have to talk about that, Gibbons."

The town-gown turf war over the Burch murder was on.

Chapter Six
A Case for McCabe

"You must be dead tired, Boss," Popcorn told me later that morning after I'd given her a quick summary of the night's events.

"I'm pretty sure I slept while I was taking a shower. I went home around five o'clock so I could help Lynda with the kids. I'm not sure how much help I was." I was tempted to ask her to poison me with caffeinated java, but fortunately the moment passed.

"Are our people and Oscar's people really going to fight about who has jurisdiction in the case?" Popcorn asked.

"Oh, they'll work it out. They need each other. Ed Decker has the surveillance video."

"That hasn't helped much in other cases Mac's been involved in."

She had a point, and a good one.

"Killers don't usually stop and smile at the camera, that's true. But the video should be of some help narrowing the field to male or female, big or small, that kind of thing. I expect we'll get the scoop on that later."

"Speaking of scoops, Hadley Reams from the *Spectator* called about five minutes before you walked in the door. He wanted to confirm that Burch was murdered."

"Already? I'm impressed. He beat the *Observer* and the Associated Press to the news. I wonder how?"

I checked my phone and saw, as expected, that Hadley had tried that number while I was on the road. I turn my phone off when I'm behind the wheel—or behind the handlebars, in this case. The state law against distracted driving is no longer limited to texting, and the fine is $100. Hadley called from the *Spectator* offices, I noted, and was probably still there.

"Instead of calling back, I'll drop in on him," I announced, pocketing the phone. "It's been months since I've been down there."

The offices of the *Spectator*, located on the lower level of Muckerheide Center, look a lot different from the early 1990s, when I edited the paper as a student. But then, what doesn't? Including me. Only the outside of Muckerheide, a horizontal concrete structure designed by a student of Frank Lloyd Wright echoing his master, hadn't changed.

Hadley Reams wasn't as skinny as he'd been when he joined the paper as a junior, and he had ditched the Trilby headgear that made him look like a refugee from *The Front Page*. He had taken to horn-rimmed glasses, though, so maybe that made up for it. His jeans were either really cheap or really expensive; I can never tell. I caught Hadley in what appeared to be rather agitated discourse with a slightly built young man with longish fair hair, wearing a high-end casual jacket and an attitude. This other student—I assumed he was a student—was taller than the aforementioned Toulouse-Lautrec, but not by a foot.

I didn't need to exercise my well-honed eaves-dropping skills to determine that they were talking about the death of Warren Burch. I didn't catch all of it, but his name came through loud and clear, along with well-worn words like "outrage" and "travesty."

"You called?" I interrupted.

Hadley stopped in mid-sentence, something about "robust reporting," and gave me his full attention.

"Hey, Jeff. I sure did. What can you tell me about the murder of Professor Burch? It's true, isn't it?"

"Yes, but how did you know? I'm guessing you weren't up listening to the police scanner this morning." And, obviously neither was Johanna Rawls at the *Observer* or Morrie Kindle of the AP.

Hadley looked canny as only a student journalist can. "I have my sources."

"The important thing is that the brightest star in this institution's firmament has been snuffed out," said the other student.

Even for a sophomore that would have been over the top rhetorical overkill, but it turned out that this was a fourth-year student.

"Meet Jason Danvers," Hadley told me, tossing a thumb in his direction. I knew that name—Burch's one-man cheering section, author of the opinion piece defending him in the *Spectator*. "This is Jeff Cody, Jason."

"Pleasure," I lied.

Danvers didn't bother to lie. He barely spared me a reluctant handshake before announcing, "I'm here to get information about the murder of Dr. Burch. I thought the *Spectator* would be plugged in."

"So, plug me in," Hadley said. "What do you know?"

"Not too much, Hadley. Burch was bludgeoned by a heavy object in his office." Dr. Eppensteiner didn't want me to give out details to the press, but that seemed vague enough to be harmless. "A campus police officer found the body sometime after eleven last night, close to eleven-thirty. The investigation is ongoing. Chiefs Decker and Hummel, or their assistants, should have more later." The results of that surveillance video, for example. "I don't speak for the Erin police, of course."

I addressed my comments to the *Spectator* editor, figuring I didn't need to schmooze Jason Danvers. Maybe I figured wrong.

"Come on, Jeff," Hadley said. "You know the cops won't tell me anything they don't tell the off-campus media. I need the inside dope. A great story could help me get a journalism job when I graduate." *Considering you're in the sixth*

year of a four-year program, you need all the help you can get, Hadley.
"What does Professor McCabe think?"

"The last time I saw Mac, the victim's body was
barely cold. I don't think he thinks anything yet, but I never
know half of what he's thinking anyway." *Nice try, though.*

"I certainly hope the university administration will
devote as much energy to finding Professor Burch's killer as
it did to destroying his reputation," Danvers said.

No, we used up all our energy on the reputation thing.

I addressed Hadley, who had his fingers eagerly
poised on his laptop keyboard. "As you know as well as
anyone, the recent spate of unfortunate stories about Dr.
Warren Burch wasn't initiated by the university. However, in
the spirit of transparency, we could do no less than
acknowledge the facts in the face of robust journalism." I was
rather proud of that, I must admit. Hadley typed.

Then I went into the part I'd worked out in my head
on the way to the newspaper office. "Dr. Burch was a
distinguished member of the St. Benignus faculty and
administration for more than four decades. While his
scholarship was notable, his true métier"—Mac loves that
word—"was classroom teaching. That was recognized when
he won the Monsignor Francis B. Kennedy Award for
Excellence in Teaching in 2005." *You don't need to know that's
what bashed his head in.* "The university mourns his loss and
looks forward to the capture of his killer."

I paused to let Hadley catch up to me. When he had,
I added, "I'm sure Father Pirelli will want to say something
later as well."

*Father Pirelli—holy crap! This was the day he planned to
resign because of Burch.* Fortunately, that train had not yet left
the station.

"But what about Professor Burch's offensive
behavior toward women in his office when he was dean?"
Hadley pressed.

"I don't think I need to say anything more about that."

And I'd better not.

"What, you don't want to back up and hit him again?" Danvers said.

Not waiting for an answer, Hadley said, "What about safety on campus? What do you say to students and parents who are afraid this campus has become dangerous?"

Ah, the old "what do you say to . . ." gambit. A favorite of journalists everywhere. Hadley had come a long way from the days when I had to sit him down and feed him the questions to ask me.

"I say, firstly, there's no reason to believe this was a random act or that anyone else was ever in danger. This heinous crime was committed in the professor's office at close quarters. That would seem to indicate that he, and he alone, was the intended victim."

"He was set up for that by the scurrilous reports of improper activity," Danvers said. "His name was widely defamed for days, while his accusers remained anonymous."

"Isn't the very fact that someone got into his office at midnight or later troubling?" Hadley piled on.

I ignored both comments. "Secondly, if you want to talk seriously about campus safety, look at the numbers. Like every college and university, SBU is required to comply each October with the Clery Act—that's the Jeanne Clery Disclosure of Campus Security Policy and Campus Crime Statistics Act—as well as the Higher Education Opportunity Act passed by Congress. That means we compile an annual security and fire safety report and post it on our website, as well as sending it to the U.S. Department of Education. It includes crimes committed on campus, on property adjacent to the campus, and on property owned by the university. If you stack up our crime stats with those of any other institution of similar size, I think you'll find they compare very favorably." *At least, I hope so.*

"I'm sure Professor Burch would be glad to know that," Danvers said acidly.

"Any other questions?" I asked Hadley.

"I'll call you if I think of any," he promised.

"Morris Kindle of the Associated Press"—as he always identifies himself—and TV4 Action News both called my smartphone number as I was walking back to my office. In between I had a check-in call from Lynda with her distinctive *Boléro* ringtone. Maggie Barton made the morning complete just a few minutes after I got back to my office.

"We heard from the cop shop that Warren Burch got done in last night," she began.

Her voice didn't sound right.

"Have you been crying?"

"Not about Burch, believe me. Death in the family."

"Oh. I'm sorry to hear that, Maggie."

"Thanks. But as for Burch, do the cops really have to find the killer?"

I'll file that under "gallows humor" and chalk it up to grief.

Just at that moment, Sebastian McCabe maneuvered his crutch-reliant way past Popcorn and into my workplace. I waved a greeting, disgusted by the clarity of his wide-awake brown eyes. He nodded. I continued my jousting with Maggie.

"Presuming you didn't call me out of idle curiosity, how come you're covering this story instead of Johanna?"

Johanna "Tall" Rawls, Lynda's leggy protégé and friend, took over the *Observer*'s crime beat when Bernard J. Silverstein succeeded Lynda as news editor. If news organizations around the country hadn't been cutting back on staff for a decade or more, she almost surely would have moved up to a bigger newspaper long ago. She was a good reporter and a good writer. Maggie's virtue, on the other hand, was that she knew everybody in town—and everybody's parents and sometimes grandparents, too.

"Oh, the dear girl will get top billing on the byline, but I offered to help out since the murder itself was on my turf." That word again—turf! Maggie lowered her voice conspiratorially. "Frankly, Jeff, I was hoping you could throw me a bone, something nobody else has."

"I could, but then I would have to kill you."

Mac raised an eyebrow in response, but Maggie laughed. She always laughs at that one, which is usually followed by me offering her something off the record. That's often helpful to keep a reporter from leaping to a wrong conclusion about some detail or other, even though he or she can't use it. It's also a way for me to bond with journalists, even in unpleasant situations where I wish they would just go away.

"Okay, can we go off the record?" I said. It's important to set the ground rules first so there can be no quibbling later. This has worked well for me over the years. No reporter has ever printed something we agreed in advance was off the record.

"Sure." The deal was sealed.

"The coroner doesn't want this out yet, but Burch was struck multiple times in the back of the head, over his right ear, by a heavy glass award."

"Award?"

"Yeah, like an Oscar, only for teaching."

"Wow—that's delicious! Are you sure I can't use it?"

"I'm sure! Don't even ask the coroner about it or I'll be on her bad side. And I don't think I want to be on her bad side."

"What else can you tell me?"

Well, there is the little matter of our president resigning, but not if I can help it.

"Nothing that Joanna won't already have from Oscar or Gibbons."

"Is Mac going to tackle this case?"

Being slightly deaf, she was talking loud enough that Mac could hear her. The expression on his face indicated the question was a silly one. I thought so, too. For one thing, he was in no position to tackle anything on those crutches.

"Why would Mac get involved?" I said. "There are already two capable police agencies on this case."

"Well, let me know when he does. How's his ankle?"

I held out the phone to him so that he could speak for himself.

"It still hurts like the very devil," he said. "Thank you for asking, Maggie."

"Sprains are painful," she informed him, as if he didn't know. "I got one skydiving a few years ago."

While they were engaging in this badinage, the Cody mind got busy. Why had Maggie moved on so quickly from the subject of the death in her family without saying who had died or how? That seemed unnatural. Suppose she really *had* been crying over Burch and didn't want to admit it. The man was less than a decade younger than Maggie, who would be called a spinster if anybody used that word anymore. She was on campus a lot, so maybe she knew Burch better than she'd ever let on. *Much* better. And maybe *that's* why she reacted so strongly to his boorish behavior with other women that it seeped into her news coverage.

At this point in the fantasy I diagnosed myself as suffering from sleep deprivation. Why else would I go down that strange path?

After a few more pleasantries, Mac handed the phone back to me and I signed off with promises to give Maggie a break when I could.

"How can you be so wide awake?" I asked the big guy.

"Caffeine, old boy."

Popcorn popped her head in the office. "Cal Daley asked you to call him back, and Father Pirelli wants you in his office right away."

"I also have been summoned by the good father," Mac said. "That is why I paid you this visit. I assumed that you had been as well, and I thought that we might walk up to his office together."

The times that Father Joe had asked me to come to his office on the double could be counted on one hand with fingers left over. And the last time had been to announce his resignation. Maybe he was going to un-announce it. But then why bring Mac into it?

"I'll call Cal after I talk to Father," I told Popcorn on our way out. Keeping her in the loop about matters big and small has become a reflex for me. No wonder Lynda calls her my office wife.

In deference to Mac's crutches, we took the elevator up one flight.

Father Joe looked like I felt. He must have slept about as much. The bags under his eyes had bags, but that didn't stop me from making the opening salvo.

"I hope you've had second thoughts about resigning," I said.

His face was one big exclamation mark. "What? Not for a nanosecond. The murder doesn't change what I did— or rather, what I failed to do."

"It is about the murder you wish to speak with us, I presume," Mac rumbled.

Amazing, Holmes! I should have known that's why Mac was part of this confab.

"That's right," Father Joe said. "It doesn't take a public relations genius like Jeff to figure out that the quicker this crime is solved the better, for the sake of the university. If a professor can be murdered in his own office with impunity, no one will feel safe on this campus. That would be disastrous. I'm just a lame-duck president, but I'm asking you to take on the case, Sebastian. It's obvious to me that your unique talents are needed."

Mac feigned surprise. "I am honored that you think so, Joseph. However, as Jefferson rightly pointed out to a veteran member of the Fourth Estate, there are already two police agencies investigating the matter with all their considerable resources."

"I'm aware of that, of course. But Lesley and I had a briefing by Cal Daley about the matter less than half an hour ago, at which learned there is an extraordinary feature making this a case for Sebastian McCabe." He didn't lean across his mahogany desk and look serious, or pause dramatically, but if this were a movie he would have. "I'm sure you know that surveillance cameras cover the building, as they do all the buildings here on campus."

"Right," I said. "Cal tried to reach me this morning, and I expected him to tell me what the video showed."

"Therein lies the problem, Jeff. The video doesn't show anyone other than Burch and Officer Jackson entering or leaving Mackie Hall at the relevant time."

"In other words," Mac said, "the murder of Warren Burch would appear to be an impossible crime."

Chapter Seven
Suspects

After that, my success in talking Father Joe into holding a news conference was almost anti-climactic. Standing in the hallway outside his office, I fired off a quick text asking Popcorn to send out the release announcing his resignation and a news conference at 2:30. Mac waited patiently.

My thoughts turned back to the murder as soon as I pocketed the phone.

"You know," I told Mac, "this impossible crime trope is so made-to-order for you that it's almost like the killer was trying to lure you into the case."

"What a delightfully devious thought, Jefferson! You have the mind of a mystery writer."

"Dozens of publishers disagree with you," I reminded him. I gave up on my Max Cutter private eye series at seven or eight unpublished novels. I can take a hint.

"However, as alluring as the 'how' of this case may be, I think it would be wiser to begin with the 'why' because that is more likely to lead to the 'who.'"

"Is this where we start listing suspects?" Mac didn't seem in any hurry to leave the Gamble Building, and this was as good a place to get into it as any.

"Why not, old boy?"

"Then we start with Mrs. Burch, of course." I remembered her as a refined woman, board chair of Erin's small but respectable Shinkle Museum of Art, where Kate is a docent. "The surviving spouse is automatically at the top of any murder suspect list, and I can't imagine this particular spouse taking Burch's unsavory behavior lying down."

Maybe that wasn't the best word choice.

Mac nodded thoughtfully. "Then there are Professor Burch's victims, the three students. By thunder, Jefferson, we are in the midst of our own 'Adventure of the Three Students!'"

Oh, no! It doesn't take a Sherlock Holmes to see where this is going.

Before I could stop him, Mac rattled off the plot of a Holmes story, something about a stolen exam paper and only three suspects. I tried to bring him back to earth.

"This is more like a matter of stolen innocence, and Burch was the thief. Are the women he harassed really valid suspects?"

He shrugged his massive shoulders. "They are certainly not to be ignored. Nor are their family members, who might be outraged on their behalf."

"I think it's more likely one of his current students killed him," I joshed. "Semester exams are coming up, and I've heard that his were torture."

Mac waxed skeptical. "If challenging examinations were a motive, no increase in campus security could protect half of my colleagues. I say that with a measure of pride, incidentally. Academic rigor is not a defect."

"What else have you got, then?"

"Surely you have not forgotten that there was a great deal of animosity toward the deceased from faculty members during his short tenure as dean, even more than usual in dean-faculty relations?"

"No, I haven't forgotten. And on that basis, you could put Dr. Esme DeVore at the top of the list as leader of the anti-Burch pack. But she and her camp got what they wanted when Burch was deposed."

"And yet he was still on the faculty, Jefferson, a daily burr in their side once he returned to campus from his negotiated sabbatical."

"That's weak. Besides, if a member of the faculty killed him, that would be bad publicity for the university. We can't have that." I thought a minute. "What about business? Burch was a business professor. Maybe he dabbled in business himself, had some partners. Those are always good suspects, just like marriage partners."

Mac nodded slowly. "Worth investigating, I grant you. However, I regret that I have to bring our speculations back to campus by reminding you that the victim had a particularly contentious relationship with the Provost."

"Saylor-Mackie? A killer? That's absurd!" *Well, we did consider her a serious suspect in another case, but never mind that. And don't tell her.*

"For you and me the notion is untenable, knowing her as we do, I grant you. Look at the situation from a law enforcement point of view, however: Lesley began the process of removing Warren Burch as dean only with great reluctance precisely because his criticism of her was well known. He contended in public that she owed her position at the university to her husband's beneficence to the School of Business and Economics, a contribution so large that it resulted in the school being named after him."

"But who could believe that Saylor-Mackie would kill him over that?"

"Yes, who?"

That wasn't Mac talking—it was Lesley Saylor-Mackie herself, just coming out of her office. She wore an elegant silver and gray shawl, nicely picking up the gray in her hair, over a black dress.

"I guess I picked a good time to see Father Joe," she said, pointing toward his end of the building. "Or would you say that I didn't?"

Well, this is a little awkward. But don't say it never happened to you that a person you were just talking about or thinking about appeared in the flesh. Although in your case you probably weren't talking about why that person could be a murder suspect.

"Ah, Lesley!" Mac bellowed. "How fortuitous! Jefferson and I were engaging in our familiar process of eliminating suspects."

"Oh, really," she said dryly.

"It's a thing we do," I confirmed. "It's kind of like brainstorming."

"It doesn't sound like much of a brainstorm to me, you geniuses. If you don't think I already got my payback on Warren by sending him back to the faculty that hated him, that's only because you don't know Warren. He was devastated by the loss of face, and his wife even more so. Are you going to ask me if I have an alibi?"

"Of course not," I said.

"At some point, however, Oscar might," Mac riposted.

The chief of police worked quite well with Saylor-Mackie during her seven years as mayor of Erin, but that wouldn't buy her anything more from him than the presumption of innocence that every citizen deserves.

"I mean, it's a waste of time to ask, even if you were a likely suspect," I clarified. "Who has an alibi for eleven-ish on a weeknight?"

"I do," Saylor-Mackie said. "I was hosting a dinner party at our home for three other couples, all generous contributors to the university. I can give you their names if you want. The soirée went well past midnight."

Mac arched an eyebrow. "Surely that is unusual."

"We were celebrating Gulliver's birthday and the other couples are all retired but not retiring. And I must admit that some of the guests needed time and coffee before they could safely drive home."

"Most prudent," Mac said. "That aside, and assuming the role of devil's advocate, I might point out that you can go anywhere on campus and scarcely be noticed—rather like Chesterton's invisible man. That would have been most advantageous in this situation."

If she weren't the refined and redoubtable Lesley Saylor-Mackie, I would have called the sound coming out of her nose a snort. "I'm flattered. I also recognize the reference. In fact, 'The Invisible Man' is one of my favorite detective stories. But at that time of night, I think even I would stand out on campus. I hope you have a better suspect."

"We don't have any suspects," I asserted. "We're just throwing around ideas, and I have to say those ideas are all pretty obvious at this point."

"Dr. Burch's colleagues on the faculty, for example, had not escaped our notice," Mac added.

"Well, I'm sure they aren't wearing black arm bands."

"If I had my way, I'd rather it's the wife," I said.

"Catherine Burch—now there's a piece of work."

Is that an academic term?

"Then there are the young women against whom Dr. Burch offended—or, perhaps more realistically—their parents," Mac said.

"I can see how they might want to hurt the man permanently, Mac, but in his office after midnight?"

"As Sherlock Holmes might have said, this case is not without its interesting features."

"Can you get us the names of the victims?" I asked.

"I already know them. Father Joe and I talked to each one to apologize after the investigation was complete. I'll never forget the names of those brave women—Amal Abood, Madison Lee, and Zoe Slade."

Something crawled up my spine.

"Slade?"

"Yes—she's Marvin and Erica's daughter."

Chapter Eight
Turf Battle

"No wonder our beloved prosecutor had such a mad-on about Burch the day we saw him at the gym!" I told Mac after Saylor-Mackie departed. If I didn't want to impose our further ruminations on her, it was for her own mental health.

Mac considered his bandaged ankle. "I have successfully repressed most memories of that painful day, but I do recall that Marvin Slade appeared more than professionally agitated. Surely, as a father you can sympathize."

Somehow, knowing the parents of one of the young women involved made Burch's assholery more real.

"Sympathize? It would have taken you to hold me back from punching the old letch's lights out permanently." From where I stood, three sets of parents—one of them the Slades—had ample motive for braining Warren Burch in the heat of the moment. But why late at night in his office? And would Burch have let somebody like that into the locked building?

I checked the time on my phone. It felt like the day was more than half over, and it was only 10:12. And I still had a news conference to referee in the afternoon.

"Well, let us not get ahead of ourselves," Mac said. "'It is a capital mistake to theorize before one has data.' Are you free to pay Oscar a call?"

The press conference would be mostly Q&A, with a brief opening statement which I wrote and expected Father Joe to gently edit with his own special touch. Nothing else was going on in the office that Popcorn couldn't handle as well or better than me, so my calendar was clear.

"Let's go," I said.

Erin's police headquarters and a small lockup with a few holding cells are located in an old art deco structure on Court Street. The building once held the Fifth National Bank of Erin, long ago absorbed into Gamble Bank. I keep hoping Oscar will do something creative with the vault, like turning it into an interrogation room, but creativity isn't his long suit.

Oscar's new administrative assistant, young Holly Burdette, winked and waved us through. We found her boss in what might be called spirited conversation with Ed Decker—two police chiefs mano a mano.

"It was on my campus," Decker asserted, not softly.

"It was in my town," Oscar said. "You didn't complain the last time I took a murder off your hands."

Decker grunted. "This one feels more personal. The victim was one of ours, and I think the killer was, too."

I slipped into an empty chair. Mac hobbled over to the Keurig machine and prepared a cup of caffeine for himself and a decaf cappuccino for me.

"Help yourself," Oscar called out. He really should leave the sarcasm to an expert—me, for instance.

Erin's top cop no longer seems like he's perpetually on the verge of a heart attack, as he did in the first few years after coming here from the Dayton force. The love of a good woman and the assurance that Mac has his back has mellowed him out quite a bit. (Oscar has gone so far as to call Mac and me "unofficial deputies" on occasion.) He also dresses better now under Popcorn's influence—no more clashing plaids or tight jackets that emphasize the bowling ball belly when he's not in uniform. I don't think he's quite so bald as the late Warren Burch, but who can tell beneath his succession of hats? I've seen him wear almost anything but a deerstalker. Today he had on his official chief's hat instead of some faux fur thing swiped off Vladimir Putin.

"I'm sorry to intrude on your conference," Mac lied. "Perhaps I can be of assistance."

"No," the chiefs said in chorus. They both knew better, but this was a master class in Face Savings 101.

"What I mean about the killer," Ed Decker went on, "is that somehow he—"

"Or she," Oscar inserted. He vaped—another Popcorn influence. My theory is that she balked at kissing an ashtray, so he takes his nicotine without tobacco these days.

Decker grunted. "Am I telling this or are you telling this? I think I'm telling this. Somehow the killer got in without setting off an alarm and without even showing up on the surveillance video. I don't know how he *or she* did it, but that smacks of an inside job to me. Besides, how would anybody from off campus know that Burch sometimes worked that late?"

"It surprised me when I first heard it," I informed them.

"Maybe Burch invited the killer to campus for a secret meeting and somehow worked out the security alarm business," Oscar posited. "He made a big mistake by turning his back on his guest."

"But the surveillance video doesn't show anybody coming *or* going!" Decker exploded.

"Maybe there's some kind of flaw in your equipment."

Ignoring that boneheaded comment, Decker turned to me. "We need to keep that under wraps. If any media types ask about the surveillance video, be vague. Just say it's inconclusive or something like that."

"Okay, Ed."

Does anybody else want to tell me how to do my job? I was still chaffing under the gag order from Dr. Eppensteiner not to discuss the weapon or the nature of the wound. She couldn't enforce it, of course, any more than Ed Decker could. But they both had ways of making life miserable for me if I didn't play it their way.

"What exactly does this inconclusive video show?" Mac asked.

"The building closes at five o'clock, when most people leave, so that's where we started studying it. The cleaning staff show up shortly afterward. Do you want the exact times?"

"Perhaps later."

I think that question was sarcastic.

"After an hour or so, Burch arrives, briefcase in hand. The cleaning crew exits the scene right after. Hours later, Burch leaves the building and comes back real quick, in maybe ten minutes, this time carrying Chinese takeout from the Golden Dragon instead of the briefcase. You know the Dragon? That's the one only about a block from campus. The video also shows Officer Jackson entering the building twice on his rounds. So, bottom line, everything Jackson said checks out."

Decker seemed to be defending his officer against unvoiced skepticism, despite the "Covering his ass?" comment the night before.

Mac set down the **I SEE NO REASON TO ACT MY AGE** coffee mug that Oscar keeps for him. "Let me recast my offer of support. I would be willing to act as a mediator or conduit between town and gown law enforcement agencies. After all, we all desire the same thing."

In theory, anyway.

Oscar shook his head. "No dice. Another cook is just what we don't need in this soup."

"I'm calling my boss," Decker said.

Mac brightened. "Give him my regards. Cal is an old friend of mine."

"His problem."

When Daley answered, Decker outlined the state of impasse at which the two chiefs had arrived. Then, he listened for a good two minutes.

"Uh-huh. Uh-huh. Okay. Absolutely clear, sir. Good-bye." Decker disconnected, then told his phone: "You're the boss. I'm just the Chief." He looked sullen.

"Well?" Mac asked.

"My boss has been talking to your boss, the Reverend Mayor," Decker told Oscar. "He said you should have a text message from Sutterlee."

Oscar looked down. "Hell's bells!"

Mac and I were on the outside of an inside joke that wasn't funny. "What's up, Chiefs?"

"We're under orders to work together," Oscar said. "As if we wouldn't!"

"It's kind of insulting that they think we need to be told that," Decker picked up the theme.

"*Very* insulting," Oscar topped him. "Tell you what, Ed: I'll give you my best man, Jack Gibbons, as my liaison with you on this case."

"Fine. I'll give you *my* best man, Aurelia Banfield, to liaise with *your* best man."

While they worked themselves up to burst into a chorus of "Kumbaya," I glanced down at my twitter feed and saw a tweet from Jason Danvers: *The haters got to Prof Burch, who gave his life to SBU. Working in office at almost midnight! Hope the administration is satisfied!* That was bad enough, but then came: *How safe is campus where beloved teacher murdered in his own office?*

That was hot air, but troublesome hot air that I would have to address. But for now, I focused back on what was going on in the room.

"We already have an appointment to interview Mrs. Burch," Oscar revealed. "I'm hoping she'll be in better shape than she was when she identified the body."

I wasn't sorry I missed that.

"Fine." Decker tried to sound like he was making a concession. "You can handle her and any suspects you come up with that have no connection to the university. My team will handle campus-related interviews. Gibbons and Banfield can compare notes as we go along."

"Like what campus-related interviews, for instance?" Oscar asked.

"Surely it has occurred to you that the young women whom Professor Burch offended, and perhaps even more so their parents, warrant investigation?" Mac said.

"Oh. Sure. You can't ignore them, I guess. Anybody I know?"

Chapter Nine
Cold Shoulder

Catherine Harridan Burch was old money. That didn't mean anything to me because money spends the same no matter the age, and most of mine is newer than 2008. But Oscar decided to interview her at home instead of asking her to come to the police station, and he kept his uniform hat on.

The Burches lived in a huge 1960s brick and cedar shake split-level about twenty miles outside of Erin proper, in leafy Sussex County. It must have cost a pretty penny, but it wasn't a pretty house. The widow welcomed us into a large hallway. She gripped a small lace handkerchief tightly in her right hand. I caught a whiff of Birth of Venus, the mind-altering $99-an-ounce perfume that Lynda's mother made famous.

"I'm sorry to intrude at this difficult time," Oscar assured her.

"Thank you, Chief." Her comment sounded about as perfunctory as his, delivered in a tone only slightly warmer than the outside temperature.

"And this is—"

"I recognize both gentlemen from St. Benignus, and I must say I'm surprised that you brought them here."

She managed to put the faintest irony into her enunciation of the word "gentleman," and she didn't acknowledge Gibbons.

"Think of them as unofficial deputies, not representatives of the university in this interview," Oscar said. "Gibbons here is my assistant chief."

She admitted Gibbons's existence with a nod in his direction.

Mrs. Burch was a trim, handsome woman with ash-blond hair in a blunt cut, just brushing her collar and tucked behind her ears. Her eyes, deep brown, showed tear-damage and had bags under them. She wore a navy cashmere dress, accented by a designer scarf and heirloom gold earrings that screamed Harridan family dough. Her fingernails were painted aqua. The dress had holes in the shoulders—Lynda tells me that's called the "cold shoulder" look and is very fashionable. The term seemed very appropriate for Mrs. B. I bet her spirit animal was an arctic fox. Her age must have been in the upper fifties, maybe eight years or so younger than her late husband.

"I'm sorry for your loss," I told her.

But for me she wasn't up to the niceties. "I'm sure you're much sorrier for the bad publicity."

Well, yeah, now that you mention it, I am.

"Your husband has been in my prayers," Mac said.

He needs them.

I was trying hard to think no ill of the dead – honest! – but it wasn't working.

"Can we just get this over with?" the widow asked frostily.

Before anybody could answer, a new character entered the cast.

"I'd better be on my way, Catherine."

The speaker was Adam Mendenhall, the energetic director of the Shinkle Museum of Art. I knew him casually through the artist in the family, my sister Kate. He was a little younger than me, about Mac's height but not his breadth, and a bowtie-and-suspenders guy. In nine years at the helm of the Shinkle, he had exhibited a golden touch—he knew how to put the touch on the people who had the gold. Maybe that's how Mrs. Burch wound up as his board chair.

Seeing four pairs of visiting eyes giving him the twice over, Mendenhall seemed to feel the need to explain himself. "I was just expressing my sympathy to Mrs. Burch."

Maybe puce wasn't really the best bowtie color for that sentiment, Adam. He also wore a camel-hair top coat. Mac told me later that the coat indicated his visit had been a brief one, since he hadn't gotten around to shedding the outer layer. I filed that away for future reference.

"What happened to you, Mac?" he added, eying the crutches. This is a question that gets old fast, as I know from experience.

"Football injury," I quipped.

"It was good of you to come," Mrs. Burch told Mendenhall. It was like she was handing him his hat, even though he didn't have one. "I see no reason why I shouldn't be at the board meeting later this month."

He shook her hand, then planted a social kiss on her right cheek, and left in a flurry of farewells to the rest of us.

"You might as well come into the living room," Mrs. Burch said with an air of grudging concession. This was apparently the space just vacated by her previous visitor, off to the right of the hall. It was a square room, sunken, decorated in the style known as mid-century modern. If you call that style. The walnut hi-fi set with the turntable was kind of cool, but the sofa set too low for me.

Once we'd settled ourselves, Catherine Burch staked out her territory:

"Before you ask any questions, I want to make it clear that my husband was a dynamic man, and brilliant in the classroom. Nobody knows that better than I—that's where I met him. I was his student many years ago. The university treated him shabbily, but he nonetheless remained devoted. On that, we differed. Don't expect any financial contributions from me, either to the capital campaign or in the future."

Fortunately, Institutional Advancement isn't my headache.

"Do you have any idea who killed Dr. Burch?" Gibbons asked, no doubt totally uninterested in her estate plans.

She hugged her shoulders. I made a mental note to look that up in a book on body language, but then I forgot. Maybe she was just cold, in more ways than one. "It's obvious that the girls who accused him of those nasty things hated him for some reason. Maybe his academic standards were too demanding for them."

"You do not believe their accusations?" Mac asked.

"Of course not. And I'll tell you something else: That administrative assistant of his when he was dean, Heidi Guildenstern, she coveted Warren."

Mac raised two eyebrows—probably one for her use of the rather rare word "coveted" and one for the idea that Heidi was capable of such a sin.

Gibbons made a note.

"Any other suggestions?" Oscar asked.

"No."

"No other women who—"

"No."

"According to the night security officer, Professor Burch occasionally worked late hours on campus," I said. "Is that true?"

"Yes, at times. He didn't bring academic work home as a matter of personal preference. His office here at home was devoted to various business interests rather than his professional ones. Just now he was working on an article about the role of central banks in the Great Recession. That's why he was on campus that night. He wanted to finish the article before we headed off to our home in Florida at the end of the term."

"Who knew about this habit of sometimes putting in late hours at SBU?"

"I have no idea."

"Did you wait up for him?" Mac asked.

"I think I woke her up when I called," Oscar said.

"That's right. I went to an opening at the Looney Ladies Gallery, came home by ten, and went to bed."

"Does it surprise you that your husband ordered Chinese takeout late in the evening?" Mac said. *Again with questions about the takeout!*

"Not at all. I didn't cook last night because I had finger food at the gallery. And he sometimes didn't eat until very late when he was working on something." She almost smiled. "He liked General Tso's chicken."

"About those business interests you mentioned. What was their nature?"

"Warren invested in stocks and bonds, just like anybody else." *I hope he stuck to index mutual funds; that's the best bet for the long haul.* "But he also believed so strongly in small business that he was a silent partner in a number of them here in town. He regarded that as a social enterprise on his part, much more about helping the community than making money."

In a similar vein, perhaps, Mac is the so-called "silent partner" in Mo's Mysteries & Marvels mystery and science fiction bookstore, although I've never heard him call it a "social enterprise." Whether Burch's investment was as altruistic as his wife thought was up for grabs. But it wasn't impossible. Nobody is all bad, I reminded myself.

Gibbons looked up from his notebook. "Do you know the names of these local businesses?"

"Warren kept me fully informed." Her tone suggested the question was a silly one. "He held an interest at one time or another in A Touch of Glass, Wine Not, Canine College, Vaporize, Black & White, and Dust to Dust. I'm sure that he cashed out on some of those, but I don't remember off-hand which ones."

"Worth looking into," Gibbons muttered.

"I hope that it will not be too long before your husband's personal items are returned to you from his office—his teaching awards and so forth," Mac told Mrs. Burch. "The Kennedy Award, for example."

Gibbons looked up at that.

"Yes," she said in a low, vague voice, "I would like to have them."

She put her right fist up to her mouth, still gripping the handkerchief as she had when she'd come to the door.

Chapter Ten
No Flowers for the Dead

"What the hell was that about the dead guy's personal effects?" Oscar demanded as we prepared to go our separate ways from the Burch house.

"His wife's reaction to that mention of teaching awards was muted," Gibbons pointed out. "The killer, but only the killer, would know that Mac was talking about the murder weapon. That didn't appear in the press. If Mrs. Burch showed a strong emotion, that might have been an indication she knew the deadly significance of the Monsignor Francis B. Kennedy Award."

"Precisely," Mac confirmed. "Of course, she might have been prepared for some reference to the fatal instrument. Her lack of response cannot be considered definitive." Leaning on his crutches, he pulled out his smartphone and began giving his thumbs a workout.

"Oh." Oscar turned to Gibbons. "Well, what next, Jack?"

"I'm going to poke around a little bit into those businesses Burch was invested in. See if any of them are in trouble. Partners in businesses usually insure each other." I nodded sagely. We'd been down that road in the opera murders. "Or it could go the other way—maybe a rival business would like Burch out of the picture. Seems to me that Hawes & Holder, for instance, might be feeling a little pressure from Dust to Dust, that new 'natural burial' operation."

This was just the sort of dogged, routine work that the unflappable Gibbons, medium in all respects except for ability, excelled in. For my part, he was welcome to it. What were the odds that some business type was on campus late at night and somehow managed to avoid the security video? Slim to none, I'd say.

Mac looked up from his smartphone. "I have been texting your counterpart, Ms. Banfield," he informed Gibbons. "She has an interview at three-thirty with the delightful Esme DeVore in her office and has invited my participation."

I'm not sure "delightful" is the adjective I'd use for Dr. Devore.

"Who's that?" Gibbons asked. "DeVore, I mean."

"Warren's bête noire on the faculty."

"His biggest pain in the ass when he was dean of the business school," I translated. "She engineered the faculty vote of 'no confidence' because of his administrative style even before his bad behavior with students came to light."

"I trust you will join me, Jefferson?"

"Maybe. If I have time. After lunch I have to help Father Joe meet the press."

We set up the news conference in a small auditorium in the Gamble Building. We probably could have done it in Father Joe's office, but I wanted to make sure we had plenty of room for any regional media that were drawn by the murder. As it happened, the Fourth Estate crowd was a small one—Maggie Barton, Morrie Kindle, Mandy Peters of TV4 in Cincinnati, and campus media. Hadley Reams wore a sport coat over his jeans.

At precisely 2:30 I stepped to the microphone, thanked everybody for coming, and got out of the way. Father Joe replaced me at the podium, sans his trademark smile. He wrote his remarks without input from me, a rarity.

"I want to begin by saying how personally sorry I am about the murder of a long-time member of the St. Benignus family, Professor Warren Burch. I said my morning Mass today for the repose of his soul. I am praying for his family as well. The St. Benignus University Police Division is working with the Erin Police Department to bring his killer to justice as soon as possible.

"That is really the most important thing on my mind this afternoon, but it is not the reason for this news conference. I made a very poor decision last year by not taking stronger measures in response to Professor Burch's totally inappropriate behavior with three female students. If I can no longer trust my own judgement, I can't expect the university community to do so. Therefore, I have decided to resign at the end of this term, which comes next week."

They already knew that—it was in the press release—but now that he said it, they could get in their questions. They were mostly softballs. I'll just hit some highlights.

MAGGIE: "When did you reach this decision?"

FATHER JOE: "Over the weekend I considered it so seriously that I informed the chairman of our board of trustees. I took it to prayer and made the final decision on Monday. I told key members of my staff yesterday."

I could see the wheels turning as Maggie realized that her story was indeed the precipitator of this momentous changing of the guard at SBU.

MAGGIE: "But doesn't Burch's death change things?"

FATHER JOE: "Not at all."

HADLEY REAMS: "Many students and parents will be worried about campus security. What do you say to reassure them?"

FATHER JOE: "I'm confident in Calvin Daley, our Director of Public Safety. Nevertheless, one of my last acts as president will be to order creation of a task force to perform a top-to-bottom review of campus security to make sure we're doing everything that can be done. Members of the task force will include all elements of the university community, notably students."

I tweeted: *"Fr Pirelli orders SBU campus security audit as one of last acts before stepping down."*

MANDY PETERS: "What accomplishment as president are you proudest of?"

FATHER JOE: "I didn't accomplish anything as president." (I winced, hoping TV4 Action News didn't cut off the quote there.) "I was just the conductor of the symphony. Others did the real work. I'm proud that we've been able to grow, thrive, and maintain our Catholic identity over the past three decades."

MORRIE KINDLE: "What's next—for you and for the university?"

FATHER JOE: "I plan to read a lot and write a little. It might be a good idea for me to relocate, but I haven't decided. The board of trustees will meet tonight and choose an interim president."

I would have a long evening ahead, attending the board meeting and cranking out a late-evening release on the results.

Predictably, after the last question was asked the perfectly-coiffed Mandy Peters begged for a few minutes to do a two-shot with Father Joe (reporter and subject in the same frame) and then a few minutes of B-roll (film to be used without sound) at his desk. She handled the camera herself, staffing being what it is in TV news these days.

Mandy was out the door by 3:15.

"How did I do?" Father Joe asked.

"I couldn't have done it better myself," I assured him. He had the grace to look pleased at what could have been taken as an ambiguous comment.

After a brief stop in my office so Popcorn didn't forget what I looked like, I hoofed it over to the Gulliver Mackie School of Business and Economics. Mac and his crutches stood in front of the entrance of the federal-style building (formerly known simply as "Business") with Aurelia Banfield. She looked very business-like in uniform, with her long hair tucked up under her cap.

"Ah, Jefferson, there you are," Mac said. *I'm always wherever I am.* If somebody else said that, he'd say it was illogical.

Banfield greeted me with an Afghanistan-veteran grip of a handshake.

"We were just talking about Ms. Banfield's counterpart on the Erin force," Mac said.

"I'm looking forward to working with Assistant Chief Gibbons," she said. "I've heard a lot about him."

"He's a great cop," I said, "but I don't imagine he's much of a dancer."

"I don't do much dancing anymore myself." Despite the twinkle in her baby blues, I felt like I'd stuck a particularly big foot in my mouth. She moved so well on her prosthesis that I'd forgotten she lost a leg in action.

"What I mean is," I hastened to clarify, "he's rather focused."

"So am I."

I believe it.

"Thank you again for inviting us to sit in on the interview," Mac told her.

"I'll be interested in your take, but it's my interview."

"Of course."

"I mean, I ask the questions."

"That is understood."

But not believed.

"Incidentally," Mac added, "I received a phone call from Johanna Rawls asking me if I were involved in the case. Candor compelled me to acknowledge a tangential role, at the sufferance of the two highly capable police agencies involved. My sense of our conversation was that with her colleague Maggie aggressively pursuing coverage for the *Observer*,

Johanna is eager to assure that her journalistic role in the story is more than peripheral."

"Wow," Banfield said, "hanging around you is going to increase my vocabulary, if nothing else."

Esme DeVore greeted us with a posture that sent an unspoken message: we shouldn't have been two minutes late—and we shouldn't have been "we."

"I wasn't expecting a whole posse," she said.

"If our presence makes you uncomfortable—"

"I'm used to uncomfortable. Didn't St. Teresa of Avila call life a night in an uncomfortable inn?"

Before Mac could confirm that, and maybe throw in a few quotes from St. John of the Cross, Banfield hastened to say:

"Well, anyway, thanks for agreeing to talk to us about Warren Burch."

"I shall shed no crocodile tears, my dears." I could believe that. DeVore was somewhere past the age of Medicare eligibility, with short gray hair and a smoker's voice. What her face lacked in beauty, it made up in character. She taught ethics. After a successful turn as an accountant and savings and loan board member, like her mother before her, she had launched a second career as an academic. Her stated goal was to mentor young women who aspired to business careers. "I'm proud I helped to grease the skids for Warren."

"Not a fan," Banfield commented.

"Hardly."

"Somebody must have liked him: He got to be dean."

"It's one of the peculiarities of academia, Ms. Banfield, that the only way to advance is to be removed from what you do best. He was a good teacher and a demanding one, if the student evaluations are any indication, but he was a horrible dean. The authority went to his head and he became a petty tyrant. Look at the way he humiliated his female students. He didn't treat the faculty much better, though I have to admit that there he was an equal opportunity bully: He ran roughshod over faculty of both sexes."

"Did you put Maggie Barton on to the harassment accusation against him and the university investigation?" I didn't plan to ask that; it just slipped out. Banfield gave me a withering look, or as close to one as she could manage on her naturally friendly countenance.

DeVore shook her head. "I think it was his administrative assistant, Heidi Guildenstern." Mac raised an eyebrow. "Word in the business school was that she was smitten with him, but he thought she was a piece of furniture. She must have been too old to catch his roving eye. So— woman scorned and all that. Don't look at me like that, Ms. Banfield. I know that sounds terribly old-fashioned, but I've seen it all."

I take it back. Esme DeVore is rather delightful. She could be a character in a hard-boiled detective novel—as the protagonist.

"Speaking of word on campus," she added, "I heard that Father Joe is resigning."

The old university grapevine!

"It's true," I said. "I just came from a press conference." I figured that didn't count as horning in on the interview.

"That's too bad. He's a great man."

"It's his way of punishing himself for not and firing Burch."

"Isn't that just like him? Such integrity! I'm not sure I would have done that—and I teach ethics."

"I would have thought you'd be pleased that Father Pirelli took responsibility."

DeVore looked like she needed a cigarette. I knew that look. "I wanted Burch out as dean, okay? But if Father Joe had Lesley fire him, SBU would have been hit with a lawsuit before he could clean out his desk. That would have been messier for sure, and probably more expensive as well."

That's what I thought! "One could argue that there's a principle involved, but we live in a fallen world that requires one to rise above principle on occasion."

Oh, yes, I like this woman.

I don't know what Mac was thinking as he stroked his beard, but it probably had nothing to do with the murder. Maybe he was meditating on the fallen world.

"If nobody minds," Banfield said, "I'd like to get us back on track here. It seems most likely that Professor Burch's killer was a member of the campus community. Just for the record, was it you?"

DeVore's smile was strained. "If I had a gun, I wouldn't waste a bullet on Warren Burch."

Ouch.

"Can you think of anyone else who might have wanted to kill him?" Banfield pressed.

"I've already mentioned Heidi Guildenstern. But really and truly kill him rather than destroy him? No, I can't imagine."

Chapter Eleven
The New Guard

The special SBU board of trustees meeting that night lasted until 9 P.M. I would tell you all about it, but then I'd have to kill you. If you didn't die of boredom first. The upshot was that board members elected their chairman, Grant Kingsley, as interim president for the rest of the 2018–19 academic year. They tapped fellow trustee Sister Jacinta Harrington, the über-competent president of St. Hildegarde Health, as head of the search committee to find Father Joe's permanent successor.

Kingsley, familiarly known as "GK," looks like a general in a movie—iron-gray hair closely cropped, gunmetal eyes, ramrod-straight posture, and a military physique. But he only made it to colonel while teaching for 27 years at the Air Force Academy in Colorado as part of the Behavioral Sciences and Leadership Department. The "leadership" part was his specialty. He retired to the Altiora Corp., a major defense contractor with large operations in Erin. You wouldn't think Altiora could spare its senior vice president for six months or more, but the civic-minded company granted him a leave of absence.

"GK should be a good fit," I told Lynda, herself a military brat. "He knows his way around campus. He even taught as an adjunct in the business school under Burch."

But I didn't tell her that until breakfast. After the board meeting, I had to write a press release stressing GK's tenure on the board and his crucial work on the capital campaign. This was familiar territory to me because a few emails laconically signed /*gk* had been forwarded my way. By the time I got home to Campion Lane, Lynda was sleeping the sleep of an exhausted mother of three kids under the age of three. Before I joined her in our marital bed, I detoured through the family room, where five stockings hung by the chimney with care for St. Nicholas Day, December 6. St. Nick had filled mine with tangerines, granola bars, and dark chocolate. I put a bottle of Cleopatra VII, her favorite scent, in Lynda's.

The top of Thursday morning's wood pulp edition of the *Erin Observer & News-Ledger* carried a full account of the murder, with Johanna Rawls and Maggie Barton sharing a double byline. **CONTROVERSIAL PROF SLAIN**, the headline screamed.

"You can't say it's inaccurate," Lynda pointed out amid the morning breakfast-table melee. Her curls were a bit in disarray, but she looked scrumptious in a curve-hugging ribbed turtleneck the color of milk chocolate.

"That doesn't help," I grumbled. "This is a whole new level of bad publicity."

"Well, don't be too hard on Maggie for just doing her job. She just lost her great-niece—Mallory. Overdose. You know how close Maggie is to all her nieces and nephews and their kids. She must be shattered."

"Mallory Lambert? Didn't she play basketball for SBU a couple of years ago?" I had a vague memory that she'd suffered a career-ending injury on the court.

"Right."

"Sad." That must have been the family death Maggie mentioned on the phone yesterday, and the cause of demise was the reason she didn't say much about it. That made real-world sense after a good night's sleep, unlike yesterday's fleeting pipedream that Maggie had what Mac would call an *affaire de cœur* with Burch. "Maybe family trouble is why Maggie's been off her game lately. On the other hand, maybe she should just count the candles on her last birthday cake and follow Father Joe out the door."

Murders on campus put me in a grouchy mood.

Several paragraphs of the story had Tall Rawls's fingerprints, including the one that said "SBU professor and sometime-sleuth Sebastian McCabe is assisting Erin and campus police with their inquiries." She quoted him briefly.

Maggie's story on our eminent president's surprise resignation also claimed a big chunk of page-one real estate, with a smiling photo. It was a nice piece, very personal, with warm anecdotes from her years of covering the great man. Each of Maggie's SBU stories referred to the other, which was inevitable given that the late Warren Burch's depredations had precipitated the Pirelli departure.

The news that GK was stepping into those big shoes was too late for the print edition, but the *Online Observer* had a quick-and-dirty re-write of my late-night press release. ("Grant Kingsley, 58, Erin-based senior vice president of the Altiora Corp., has been named . . .") I happened to know that GK played golf with Frank Woodford, editor and general manager of the *Observer*. But then, who didn't? "Community engagement" was Frank's specialty, while he left the running of the paper to Ben Silverstein.

"Want to hear your horoscope, darling?"

"No."

She read it to me anyway:

"'The real challenge will be in choosing what to believe.' Hey, that's not bad for an amateur sleuth! Mine says, 'Productivity and joy go hand in hand.'" She looked at our three children, the result of our productivity in marriage. "Well, that's certainly true!"

Father Joe's office—*former* office—somehow looked smaller with him not in it.

"He's gone already?" I marveled. "His resignation isn't official until Sunday night." This was perhaps not the best opening line for my first meeting with my boss's boss. But I was shocked into it. I expected that Father Joe would be there along with the new guy.

"He'll be back later today," GK reassured me. "He insisted that I use the president's office today for my first team meetings—symbolism and all that. Who am I to argue with Father Joe? But I'm not going to move in here for another week. I can work out of my briefcase until then. And after that, Father Joe will get an office on this floor as President Emeritus. *I* insisted on that. He can share my administrative assistant when he's not hitting the links."

"That's very sensitive of you," said Lesley Saylor-Mackie. She'd had GK to herself for an hour before they invited me into the confab. Not that it was an invitation I could refuse.

The interim president pressed beyond the matter of his predecessor's digs, a man in a hurry.

"I want to meet as many key people as I can today, Jeff, and you are one of the key people. I've always believed that good communication is essential to good leadership. So, your office will be essential to whatever I do in this transition period."

I like this guy.

"Even though I'll be a short-timer behind this desk, I'm not going to just take up space. My motto is 'leaders lead.' I'm going to push forward with the capital campaign, for starters. Father Joe will be very important as the face of that. Everybody knows him, everybody loves him. Day to day, you can expect me to be a little stronger hand at the rudder than he's been, without micromanaging."

That wouldn't be hard. Father Joe's laissez faire management style was the reason "Executive Vice President" was part of Saylor-Mackie's rather cumbersome title. You don't get rid of an institutional legend; you work around him.

"Naturally," GK continued, "I'm very concerned about Warren's murder. Hell of a thing to face on my first day!"

"All downhill from here," I joshed.

"Not necessarily." That bucket of cold water came from Saylor-Mackie. "All indications are that the killer is a member of the St. Benignus community, not an outsider."

"That's what worries me—that and the whole campus security issue." GK sat back, looking comfortably at home behind the presidential desk. As his suit coat parted, I saw a wrapped cigar in his shirt pocket. "I've been fully briefed by Chief Hummel as well as by our own people." *This guy works fast!* "I made a few calls before the board meeting yesterday. I'm also aware of what's out there in social media. Somebody named Jason Danvers tweets more than Donald Trump."

"He was close to Burch," I said.

"I figured that, but he's taking so many pot shots at safety on campus that they're bound to hit home with some people. Can't we do anything about him, Jeff?"

"In short, no. Ralph Pendergast, of blessed memory, would want us to fire back at him. That's the worst possible reaction, in my considered opinion. It would call attention to his rantings, and thereby give him a bigger stage than if we just ignore him. Other professionals might argue differently, but that's what I think."

"Hmm. I guess you're right. Well, Father Joe was wise to order that safety review. I've stressed to Cal Daley that I want a thorough job on that, not just a light coating of paint. He asked me if he could hire some outside talent and I gave him the green light."

"Okay to tell the press about that?"

"Sure, if they ask about the review. That can only add to the credibility of the process. And by the way, Cal also authorized overtime for extra patrols on campus at least until the killer is caught."

I made a mental note to call Hadley Reams and Maggie Barton, both of whom had asked questions about the nature of the security review yesterday.

"From where I sit"—*in Father Joe's chair*—"this murder is more than just a PR problem for SBU. Warren was something of a small 'f' friend of mine. I got him appointed to the Altiora board because I thought he brought an interesting perspective that none of the other twenty board members had. He was head of the audit committee—although, confidentially, I'm not sure he would have survived the negative publicity about the reasons he left the deanship."

"Of course, it's more than *just* a PR problem," Saylor-Mackie said. "But it would be foolish to deny that it's bringing us a lot of negative attention right on top of Warren's Title IX issue. The best thing for the university would be a quick arrest, which nobody in this room has any control over. But I'm sure all the law enforcement people are doing their best on that."

"With the help of Sebastian McCabe, I suppose?" Was that a twinkle in GK's gunmetal gray eyes? "I love his Damon Devlin mysteries." *Nobody's perfect.* "Introduce us sometime, Jeff."

"Sure. As a matter of fact, Father Joe did ask Mac to stick his beard into this case. You're copacetic with that, I gather?"

GK didn't respond as affirmatively as I expected, given that he was a self-proclaimed McCabe devotee. "I only have one caveat about it. We already have two police forces and an energetic coroner involved. From a business management point of view, somebody better be making sure they aren't stepping all over each other's toes." Only he really didn't say *toes*. "I know you're plugged in, Jeff. Are there any suspects?"

"Quite a few."

Chapter Twelve
Heidi Ho

"What do you think of our new interim president?" Mac asked.

"I think he's the right man in the right place at the right time," I opined. "He's been a military guy, an academic, and a businessman. Lots of different skill sets there. Are you sure you want to be in on the interview with Heidi Guildenstern?"

"I do not look forward to it, I assure you."

Heidi, an impassive, big-boned woman with a penchant for throwing the rule book at anybody who violated it, spent several purgatorial years as the administrative assistant for Mac's popular culture program. Almost hell, that is, both for her and for everybody that crossed her path, especially Mac. It would be hard to say whether she or Mac was happier when she was transferred across campus five years before and not replaced in a cost-saving move. At the same time, Popcorn got promoted to my assistant. As I said at the time, win-win.

Heidi had worked for Burch during his entire short tenure as dean and stayed on with his successor. She was now on the cusp of retirement, according to the campus gossip Popcorn picked up. Both her long tenure at SBU and her snow-white hair, which she wore in a pixie cut, testified that she was old enough.

"I don't see how I can help," she told Aurelia Banfield. The three of us sat around a table in a small conference room just off the dean's office in Mackie Hall.

Heidi's tone of voice indicated puzzlement rather than resistance. Maybe she intended it that way.

"Maybe you can't," Banfield conceded, woman to woman. "This is just routine."

More sartorially laid-back than when she worked for Sebastian McCabe, Heidi wore black corduroy slacks and a purplish blouse with a hint of pizzazz. She even had a silver chain around her neck. Maybe this was her pre-retirement mode. But she sat erect as ever.

"Do Professor McCabe and Mr. Cody have to be part of the routine?"

"I'm afraid so." Banfield looked sympathetic. And cute! But not lovely like Lynda. "Father Joe requested it. Just ignore them."

"Gladly." This was progress—Heidi showing a sense of humor. Mac and I weren't supposed to ask questions anyway. "I'm happy to cooperate, of course, but I've barely spoken to Dean Burch since he returned to campus."

Did her voice soften, her washed-out gray eyes tear up, at the mention of his name? Not that I could tell. But, then, she'd never been outwardly emotional. She didn't even register pleasure at the sight of Mac on crutches.

"It's possible that the motive for his murder traces back to his time as dean," Banfield said. "It would be fair to say that was a controversial period in his career." *Nicely put!* "Did you observe him engaging in questionable behavior with young women at that time?"

There was nothing relaxed about the way she shook her head to that notion. "No. I had absolutely no idea. My first intimation was when Janet Fischer"—our HR director, and one of the two investigators of the claims against Burch—"asked me questions about it. She was following up on a complaint from—Is this completely confidential?"

Now she looked at Mac and me.

"Of course," Banfield assured her.

"Ms. Fischer was following up on a complaint from a student named Madison Lee who interned as office assistant to the dean. I told her, Ms. Fischer, that I never saw anything like that. But as we talked, I realized that Dean Burch often found things for me to do out of the office when interns and work-study students were there. I suggested that Ms. Fischer might want to talk to Amal Abood. She was a work-study student who seemed desperately unhappy and transferred to another school after just one semester."

Abood was another of the three students cited by the HR director and the dean of students in their report.

"The investigators concluded that Warren Burch instilled a climate of fear, intimidation, and bullying, among the faculty as well as among the female students who worked for him," Banfield noted. "That doesn't sound like winning friends and influencing people. Can you think of anybody who particularly hated him?"

Here's a copy of the campus directory.

I could almost see Heidi's brain waves doing calisthenics as she tried to parse the response in her head before letting it come out of her mouth. "He was rather forceful with faculty members and there was a lot of pushback from those who had their own way under Dean Simmons."

"Such as?"

This is work.

"Obviously you want me to name names. All right, then. It's no secret that Professor DeVore led the charge that resulted in a faculty vote of 'no confidence' in his leadership as dean."

We'd come full circle—DeVore fingered Heidi, Heidi fingered DeVore.

"How did you feel about Professor Burch?" Banfield asked.

"I admired him very much. He held to rigorous academic standards, unlike some of my previous superiors."

Who could that be?

Heidi kept her eyes on Banfield, studiously avoiding Mac.

"And on a personal level?"

"To me personally he was never anything less than professional."

"Or anything more?" This was a question Mac had planted with Banfield.

Heidi started as if she had been punched. "What? What are you suggesting?"

"I'm not suggesting anything, Ms. Guildenstern. I'm a police officer asking a question."

"Your question has an implication that I resent. Dean Burch and I had a good working relationship, nothing more. That never led me to believe he was anything other than a gentleman with women. Frankly, I was disappointed to find out he wasn't the man I thought he was."

"Disappointed enough to tell Maggie Barton?" Mac asked.

Or did you tell her in revenge for Burch's ignoring you while he was looking up other women's dresses?

Banfield glared at Mac.

"Did she say that I did?" Heidi asked.

"By no means," Mac admitted. "I am quite sure she would never betray a source. No, that was merely conjecture on my part."

"I should have known." She sighed. "I guess it can't hurt now. Yes, I told Ms. Barton. When Dean Burch came back to campus, I would see little reminders of him here and there—his name in the minutes of departmental meetings, things like that. It bothered me more than I anticipated that he was a continuing presence here and the women that he mistreated are gone."

Banfield looked at Mac as if trying to read his mind for any additional questions he wasn't allowed to ask.

"Well," she said finally, "I think there's just one more thing. Do you know of any further victims of Professor Burch's improper attentions, I mean beyond the three that the university interviewed?"

She hesitated. "I really don't feel comfortable speculating about that. Aren't three students enough?"

"Too many," Banfield said.

Too many victims, yes—but maybe not enough suspects, I thought.

Chapter Thirteen
Reluctant Witness

"Well, what do you think, Jefferson? Did Heidi covet her neighbor's husband?"

"Fifty-fifty chance on that," I said.

Banfield gave the two of us a "you-guys-have-three-heads-each look." "Of course, she did. And I'd say it took all of about a week for her to realize that wasn't going anywhere."

Mac and I looked at each other and shrugged our shoulders.

"Does that mean you regard her as a suspect or discard her as a suspect?" Mac asked Banfield.

"Too early to say, but the betting is this was a crime of passion and she doesn't strike me as the passionate type."

"On the contrary, I know from working with her that Heidi is quite passionate about her view of how the university—and world, for that matter—ought to work. I constantly infuriated her by failing to meet her standards. However, she was never anything less than controlled."

"And controlling, if possible," I put in.

"So, if she killed somebody," Banfield said, "it would have been planned."

"I believe so," Mac said. "Of course, Professor Burch's murder could have been planned to look like it was spur-of-the-moment." This kind of double thinking always gives me a headache. "I speak only theoretically, of course. I find it hard to imagine Heidi Guildenstern as a murderess, although I have been surprised before. I think we need to talk to the objects of Professor Burch's deplorable attentions. I wish Heidi were less discreet about naming others beyond the three students we know about."

My phone made a noise. Incoming! *talking to fr joe late today for alumni mag story,* Lynda texted. *may not be home when you get here. polly will watch the 3 amigos.* Triple M—Sister Polly—may be a religious sister, but she's also an Army veteran. She would have those kids saluting by the time I got home. I texted back good luck wishes, husbandly comments of a romantic nature, and emojis of a smiley face with two hearts for eyes and a pair of lips. We also agreed to meet on campus at the end of the workday.

Mac observed my feverish typing. "Media inquiries, Jefferson?"

"The work never ends."

The first interview Banfield had set up was with Amal Abood, now a senior at another small school in New Boston, Ohio. She would meet us at her part-time job in a restaurant. New Boston was a little less than an hour and a half drive east from Erin on U.S. 52, the Ohio River Scenic Byway. Banfield piloted us in her cruiser as if alert for land mines, which reminded me that her left leg was made of plastic and metal. The sun shone brightly, and so did Banfield.

"May I smoke?" Mac asked.

"In your dreams, Seb." That dealt with, she moved on. "Ms. Abood is what you might call a reluctant witness." If she hadn't had her hands on the wheel, she probably would have put air quotes around "reluctant witness."

"How so?" Mac said. He sat in the front. I sat in the back with his crutches.

"She doesn't want anything to do with St. Benignus. At first she refused to cooperate."

"How did you persuade her?"

"I told her she could talk to me or Assistant Chief Gibbons." She smiled. "I was betting she wouldn't know what a gorgeous hunk of male we're talking about here."

Hunk? L. Jack Gibbons? Well, maybe. I guess.

"You said 'reluctant witness,' but she isn't actually a witness in the murder investigation, is she?" I said. "She's more like a suspect."

"That's something else she doesn't know."

We tossed around a few ideas here and there that didn't amount to much, then talked about some of Banfield's battlefield experiences and some of ours poking our noses where they didn't belong. We'd all seen too many dead bodies.

"So, tell me everything you know about Jack Gibbons," she said, trying to sound casual and failing miserably.

"We don't know jack about him," I quipped.

"Come on, dudes. Give. You've worked with him on cases for years. I bet you know everything important about him."

"He is unmarried and unattached," Mac said.

"See, I was right. You know everything important about him."

This sounded serious. I started texting Popcorn, then erased it. It wouldn't be fair for Gibbons to be the last to know he was in the archer's crosshairs.

"I want to start my own restaurant," Amal Abood said in excellent English. "That's why I am pursuing a degree in entrepreneurship."

We met her in the back room of a Middle Eastern café in downtown New Boston where she was about to start her shift waiting on tables to help pay her tuition. The café featured belly dancing on Saturday nights, as graphically advertised on posters. No need to mention that to Lynda.

Ms. Abood was part of a phalanx of international students drawn to SBU by Ralph Pendergast's strategic targeting of that population when he was provost. (He also added online courses and new majors in biomedical sciences and health and wellness to better compete in the academic marketplace. No flies on Ralph.) Her family had been driven out of Damascus by ISIS in 2014. She was short, with long, midnight-black hair and large brown eyes.

"You must have been very disappointed by your work-study experience with Dean Burch," Banfield said after the preliminaries were checked off.

"I regarded that as a road bump not a roadblock," the interviewee said.

Mac raised an eyebrow, impressed with the turn of phrase.

"That's what my advisor says," she explained. "She's pretty good with words. Anyway, it was a bad experience, but not the worst of my life by a long way."

DA-da-da-da—DA-da-da! That was my smartphone, belting out the Indiana Jones ringtone that I assign everyone but Lynda ("Boléro") and Mac ("You're so Vain"). Hadley Reams was calling. Damn! I'd forgotten to call and assure him and Maggie about GK's commitment to the campus safety review, even approving the hiring of outside help. I can't remember everything! Nevertheless, Hadley could wait. I declined the call.

"This was three years ago that you transferred out of SBU—after the fall semester in 2015, wasn't it?" Banfield said.

She nodded. "That's right."

"But you didn't file a complaint then." Banfield had studied the investigators' report—maybe memorized it, for all I knew.

"No. I just wanted to get out of there and move on. Besides, he was the dean and I am a woman from Syria. I didn't even have any friends on campus. But when Ms. Fischer called me and said that I could help other women, make it so nobody else would go through the humiliation I suffered, I told her what Dean Burch did to me."

"I realize the details must be embarrassing to talk about."

Amal Abood didn't look embarrassed. At that moment she looked like somebody who could take me on in a fair fight, never mind that she was about a foot shorter than me and female. "He asked me to stand on a chair to adjust an air vent in the ceiling whenever I wore a dress, then he would look up my dress. I stopped wearing dresses. Then he would drop books and ask me to pick them up while he watched me from behind. It was degrading. Once he gave me an SBU Lady Dragons T-shirt as a present and asked me to try it on. I could see it would be very tight-fitting across my chest, so I refused. He got very upset and said I was ungrateful."

If I read Banfield's body language correctly—and I did—Burch was lucky to be dead.

"Do you know anybody else he did these things to, other than the other two students who are on record?"

"No. I don't even know who the other two were. I haven't been in contact with anybody at SBU since I left."

"You must have been very angry at Warren Burch," Banfield said. "I know I would be."

"Only at first. Now I am grateful to him."

"I don't understand." *That makes at least two of us, Aurelia.*

"What he did to me became a motivation, like everything bad that has happened in my life. It all makes me determined to realize my dream. That is the American way, no?"

"That is the American way, yes," Mac said.

"I am doing very well now. My average is 4.0."

Maybe you should have sent Burch flowers while you had the chance. Wait a minute! It's not too late. The funeral is Friday.

"And now Dean Burch is dead," Ms. Abood added. "May he be at peace. That should have only happened on God's time."

"Have you been on the SBU campus lately?" Banfield asked. *Like, say, the night Burch was murdered?*

The answer came quickly and firmly: "No. Why would I ever go back there?"

Chapter Fourteen
More-than-Willing Witness

"What a remarkable young woman!" Mac said as Banfield drove us back toward Erin.

"Too bad we lost her as a student," Banfield added.

"Then you believe her?"

"I didn't say that, Seb, although I'm inclined to. I've got her on record as saying she hasn't been on the SBU campus. If anything turns up to the contrary, she'll have some explaining to do."

I called Hadley Reams back, putting him on speakerphone.

"I was just looking for an update on the murder," he said.

Any student journalist would, but Hadley had the added incentive of being just one semester away from looking for a newspaper job. He'd made that clear. No doubt that's why, as editor of the *Spectator*, he assigned the story to himself.

"You know I can't give you every jot and tittle of the investigation," I said, "but I can assure you that the campus and city police are both going full bore in investigating Professor Burch's murder. They are cooperating to interview people both on and off campus."

"Suspects, you mean?"

"I don't know if I'd use that word."

"Persons of interest, then?"

I looked at Banfield in the front seat for direction. She shook her head.

"I wouldn't use that word either."

"Well, what word *would* you use?" For some reason, he sounded frustrated.

"I would say they are talking to people who might know something, even though they might not know they know something." *Got that?* Banfield seemed doubtful.

"This is a very thorough investigation," I assured Hadley. "Moreover, the safety and security of the campus community is Priority One for Interim President Kingsley as he prepares to take over the reins of the university from Father Pirelli on Monday morning. In the short term, our campus police will increase their patrols. Students will get used to seeing uniformed officers around. In the long run, the comprehensive review of safety that Father Pirelli ordered will go forward with all possible dispatch."

"Do you think that will make students and their parents feel better?"

"No one will feel better, Hadley—including no one in the university administration—until this killer is caught."

What I thought then was: *Throw in a few quotes from Jason Danvers, rehash everything you wrote before, and you've got a passable story.* What I said was: "Any other questions?"

"Who's taking over Professor Burch's classes?"

"Dr. Wendy Yazane will be administering his tests next week. Longer term, as far as I know, the dean hasn't yet made the arrangements for covering his classes next semester. Popcorn can check that out for you if you need to know. I'm on the road right now." I like saying "on the road"—it sounds so dynamic.

After a few more pleasantries, I disconnected.

"With those increased patrols and all, this case is really going to cut into my social life," Banfield said with a grin. "When I'm not cruising the campus or with you guys, I'll be working with Jack. Oh, darn."

"A policeman's lot is not an easy one," Mac said.

Choosing not to join this badinage, I called Maggie and gave her essentially the same scoop I'd doled out to Hadley.

"Thanks," she said. "You're a lot more informative than Oscar Hummel."

"Well, you know dealing with the media doesn't rank high in his skill set."

"Do the cops think the murder weapon, the teaching award, may be significant? Are they looking at the students he harassed as suspects?"

"Hey, hold on. Don't forget, the murder weapon is strictly off the record for now. Orders from the coroner. If you print that, I'll get in trouble with Arly for telling you. Then I won't be so informative anymore."

Banfield kept looking at me in her rear-view mirror, no doubt fascinated by this inside view of how the sausage is made.

After a beat, Maggie said, "Got it. But are the girls suspects?"

Banfield shook her head, not that I needed the cue.

"No more than anybody else at this stage," I said. "As I said, law enforcement officials are talking to a wide range of people who might know something helpful. It's too soon to talk about suspects. Any other questions?"

"Not right now."

"Say, Maggie, Lynda told me about Mallory. I was really sorry to hear that."

"Oh, thanks. She was my favorite niece."

There was a catch in her voice at the end of the sentence. If Maggie weren't at work, she'd probably be bawling her eyes out. Maybe that's why she was at work.

"Well, hang in there," I said. "Talk to you later."

I disconnected.

"Masterful!" Mac said.

Banfield didn't seem so sure. "Clue me in here: Why did you describe the murder weapon to her off the record? If she can't use it in her story, the information's no good to her, is it?"

Time for a lesson in Practical PR 101. "There are a lot of reasons for sharing off-the-record material. Quite often I'll tell a reporter something I don't want printed or broadcast in order to warn him or her off from making a mistake—leaping to a wrong conclusion based on an incomplete picture, for instance. Journalists appreciate that. The trick is, you have to make clear up front what's off the record and what's not. And you have to be dealing with a reporter you trust. And I trust Maggie."

Even my annoyance with the old trouper at the tone of her stories about the Burch settlement didn't change that.

"But why would a reporter agree to let you give her information she can't use?" Banfield asked.

"Because she trusts me that she'll be better of knowing it than not knowing it. Besides, it must be fun for her being privy to stuff I haven't told her competitors. That puts her one up. They don't know it, but she does."

"Fascinating," Mac said.

Our next interview was by Skype with Madison Lee, who graduated from SBU in December 2016—a semester early because she is a brainbox—and immediately filed a complaint against Burch. She was now a law school student at Georgetown.

"I had an internship as office assistant to the dean," she said. "I thought that would be great. It turned out to be a disaster. I'll tell you anything about it you want to know. But all that happened a couple of years ago. What does it have to do with Burch's murder?"

Ms. Lee had dark black skin and long yellow hair, straightened. From what I could see on Mac's computer screen, she appeared to be well proportioned and well clothed in a multi-colored caftan dress. We called her up from Mac's office as a concession to his bum leg. Maybe Lee wouldn't notice the paperwork mountains or the bagpipes flopped over a file cabinet. The "Thank You For Not Breathing While I Smoke" sign remained as a relic of another time now that Saylor-Mackie had convinced Sebastian McCabe that the campus-wide smoking ban applied even to him.

"Your interactions with the victim may not have anything to do with the murder," Banfield replied, "but the victim seems to have left a lot of people behind who had reason to want him dead."

"Why? He was already punished by being removed from the deanship and returned to the classroom, where it's harder to get by with that kind of crap."

"Somebody may have thought that wasn't enough."

"Are you kidding? I bet it broke him. A man like that, titles are everything in his world."

With that kind of astute perception, I could foresee a great career in the law for this young woman.

"Do you know who else he mistreated?" Banfield asked.

Lee shook her head. "Besides Zoe Slade, no. But I always assumed there were others. Zoe warned me when I got the position. She had it before me and she told me why she transferred out. I thought she was exaggerating. How wrong was that! I wasn't there more than a week before he started asking me to reach high bookcases, calling me honey, asking me to give him dancing lessons. A couple of times he even adjusted his crotch in front of me."

TMI, TMI!

"But you maintained your internship through spring and fall semesters."

"Getting an internship in a dean's office is pretty much an honor. I thought it would look bad on my record if I chucked it."

"Then why not stay and lodge a complaint?" This was a side alley, but clearly one that had Banfield's interest.

"I figured that could really complicate my life. Instead, I took a heavy course load, worked my butt off, and was able to graduate two years ago this month."

"Then you filed your complaint."

"I got him in the end. That's what I keep telling myself." *Somebody really got him in the end.*

Banfield paused. Maybe she was adding it up. I know I was, and I presumed from Mac's beard-stroking that he was doing the same. Madison Lee had contributed no new names to the victim list, and in fact shot down the idea that any of Burch's accusers would have reason to put him on permanent sabbatical.

"Have you been back to the SBU campus since you left?" Banfield asked.

"No. Why would I? I'm over it. I wear dresses again."

Banfield turned to Mac. "Any questions?" Maybe she thought she owed him that because it was his office.

"Did you tell your parents?" Mac asked Lee.

She winced. "Not until I made the complaint. I think they were almost more upset with me for putting up with it than they were with Burch, especially Mom. She's the vice president for inclusion, diversity and equal opportunity at Licking Falls University. She read me the riot act."

Chapter Fifteen
Survivor

"Good question about the parents, Seb," Banfield said during the rump session after the Skype interview. "So, you're seeing them as suspects?"

"Parental love is a murder motive Jefferson and I have seen before.[3] However, there is still the nettling problem of how an outsider could show up on campus that late at night, enter Mackie Hall, and even avoid the video surveillance while doing so."

"Parents don't consider themselves outsiders," I objected. "They see themselves as tuition-payers, more often than not—stakeholders, if you want a fancy term." This I knew from my email in-basket. When controversy erupted, I heard from the stakeholders. "My guess is that most parents have been on campus more than once. More than a few small businesses in town depend on it."

"Points well taken," Mac conceded. "They do not solve our problem, however. Stakeholders do not get pass cards to buildings, nor are they invisible. What are your thoughts, Aurelia?"

"I think we're getting a clear idea why Mr. Burch didn't live to a ripe old age. He seems to have had a firmly established pattern of objectionable behaviors. Maybe he found ways to resume that when he returned to teaching and somebody took extreme exception, whether student or

---

[3] Non-spoiler alert: I'm not going to tell you which case.

parent. That's all I've got. Other than that, I hope Jack is having more success than we are."

"Am I the only one bothered that neither Ms. Abood nor Ms. Lee worried about protecting other young ladies from Burch's creepy attentions?" I asked. "Or at least, not enough to file a complaint while they were still students."

"Don't be too harsh on them." Banfield sounded almost scolding. "It's not unusual in cases of sexual harassment of any kind for the victim to be reluctant to report. It takes courage. It's not even easy for women in the military. And remember, these students are still young." *They seem to get younger every year.* "As a law enforcement officer on a university campus, I pay close attention to these cases. Right now, there's an investigation underway of a team doctor at Ohio State who killed himself thirteen years ago. Some of the men he groped never came forward until now, and there were more than a hundred of them."

"I take it that, like the earlier investigators of these reports, you deem the testimony of Ms. Abood and Ms. Lee credible," Mac said.

"Very."

There wasn't much else to say. Banfield and I departed Mac's quarters a short while later.

Lynda awaited me in my office, fresh from her interview with our outgoing president.

"Father Joe sure is a great guy," were the first words out of her mouth.

"Yeah. I miss him already."

We picked up whole wheat pizzas on our way home—only two, since our babysitter Triple M had to scoot off to a planning meeting for a student retreat as soon as we relieved her. By our standards, this was practically a date night. I filled Lynda in on my hard day's sleuthing as she drove.

Home on Campion Lane, she fed the twins pizza and talked while I fed myself and almost-three-year-old Donata.

She (Lynda, not Donata) regaled me with Pirelli anecdotes that even I had never heard before.

"So, I said to President Reagan, 'There you go again!'"

That was Lynda, imitating Father Joe imitating the Gipper—and quite humorously, too.

"What's on your agenda tomorrow while I slave over a hot computer at nap time, darling?" she asked as I cleared away the detritus after dinner.

"I could come home at nap time!"

She chuckled as though I were kidding. "No, really, what are you boys up to next?"

"First of all, we boys and Banfield are going to talk with Zoe Slade."

"I can see Erica as a total Mamma Bear. I'd love to be a fly on—"

Darling Donata, wearing a diaper for a change instead of being completely naked, interrupted this cliché to make an important announcement:

"My leg—my leg—my leg *wet!*"

Sam laughed as if he understood the implications of that. Jake grabbed another piece of pizza.

The next morning, Friday, we met the Slades in Erica's law office on Water Street. Downtown Erin was dressed for Christmas, with red ribbons and little white lights on the streetlamps.

In previous incarnations, the Slade Law Center had been St. Swithin's Episcopal chapel and then a trendy (but unprofitable) pub called The Sanctuary. The pub owner's loss was Erica's gain when his equity in the building became her fee for getting him out of a spot—a very big spot—of legal trouble. I love the stained-glass windows and the former bar, which is now a reception desk.

Ashley Crutcher, Erica's paralegal and my friend from the Poisoned Pens writing group,[4] showed us into the small conference room.

"Hello, officer and gentlemen."

Mac raised both eyebrows at the sight of Marvin Slade rising to greet us from the other side of an oval conference table. The billboards around town show Erica Slade with her dukes up and boxing gloves on ("I fight for you!"), fire in her violet eyes. In real life, Marvin is most often the other lawyer in the ring in his capacity as Sussex County prosecutor. If Sebastian McCabe had brought the two of them together outside of a court room, it would have qualified as his greatest trick. But it wasn't his doing.

"Surprised?" Erica said. "No more than I am."

The former gym teacher and Cincinnati Bengals cheerleader is pushing fifty, but not hard. Her shoulder-length black hair may not even be dyed. She stands about five-seven without her stiletto heels, but she is never without her stiletto heels. I know that because Lynda and I have spent many social hours with her at Bobbie McGee's Sports Bar. Today her athletic body was encased in a red dress that should have won an Emmy, set off by a beautiful necklace of Murano glass. Maybe she had a trial in the afternoon.

"To her credit, Erica thought I should be a part of this, and I readily agreed," Marvin Slade said. He paused, but nobody clapped. "After all, she's my daughter, too."

Said daughter sat between her parental units, looking like she'd rather be back at Miami of Ohio studying for the exams next week. The resemblance to her mother was inescapable, what with the dark hair and fit body. I'd never met her, but I'd heard about her over brews and burgers. I thought I remembered that she was as runner. For sure she was the child of two parents who didn't get along, which had to be tough.

---

[4] See *Rogues Gallery* (MX Publishing, 2014) and *Bookmarked for Murder* (MX Publishing, 2015).

Marvin took the initiative to introduce her to the trio of us. Mac bowed, in an amazing display of agility given his girth. He parked his crutches and we joined the Slades at the table.

"Officer Banfield—" Erica began.

"Assistant Chief."

Round One to Banfield!

"Of course." Erica looked bemused. Or pissed. Hard to tell. A good defense attorney must be a good actor anyway, so maybe she was putting on. "Marvin and I find ourselves in rare agreement"—her mouth flirted with the idea of a smile—"that our daughter has been traumatized enough. We're here to see that she doesn't get victimized all over again."

"I don't consider myself a victim," Zoe asserted in an assertive way. "I'm a survivor."

Dinner times at the pre-divorce Slade house must have been interesting affairs, what with three boxers in the ring.

"I appreciate that," Banfield said, covering both Slade women in one efficient comment. "And I'm sure you all appreciate that this is one of a number of routine interviews we have to conduct as part of our investigation of Professor Burch's murder. Are you here as Zoe's counsel, Ms. Slade?"

Too canny to give a close-the-door definitive answer, Erica said, "I'm here as her mother, for now. When I go into lawyer mode, you'll know it."

I bet.

Marvin leaned in. "Obviously, I'm here as her father, not as prosecuting attorney."

Nobody asked you. I guess he wanted to remind us that he was there.

Banfield nodded, appreciating that, too. "Obviously. I think all our roles are clear here."

"Oh?" Erica sounded unsure. "Who do Mac and Jeff represent?"

"Father Pirelli. He asked them to get involved. That's not exactly by-the-book, so I hope you don't mind." Banfield didn't wait for a comment on that before moving on. "During his time as dean, the late Professor Burch exhibited a pattern of misbehavior that may in some way be related to his death. So, I just want to check on the details of what he did. I'm sorry to have to ask you to go through that, Ms. Slade."

"That's all right."

Zoe Slade interned as Warren Burch's office assistant in the 2015–2016 school year. She transferred to Miami in the fall semester of 2016, warning her successor in the job—Madison Lee—on her way out.

"I wasn't working there long before I learned not to wear skirts or dresses," she said. She should have passed that advice on to Ms. Lee from the get-go, IMHO. "But that didn't stop him from looking down my blouse, making me bend over to pick things up, commenting on my nice ass. Which, by the way, is a nice ass."

Marvin winced at the addendum. Erica looked like she was trying not to look annoyed at her daughter.

"How did you feel about that?" Banfield asked.

"Powerless. Disrespected. Humiliated. Just what he wanted me to feel, I guess."

"Ask her how she feels in ten years," Erica suggested.

"Is it true that you never filed a complaint about any of this with the university?" Banfield asked Zoe.

"Yes." Zoe nervously fingered the buttons of the blue sweater she wore over a white blouse.

"Did Dean Burch threaten you or in any way prevent you from filing a complaint?"

Mac smiled his approval at this new line of inquiry, clearly designed to establish whether Burch might have pushed somebody and got pushed back hard. The question must have just occurred to Banfield since she hadn't asked either of the other women.

"No, he didn't."

"Then why didn't you file a complaint?"

"Is this an investigation or an inquisition?" Erica asked.

But her daughter didn't mind answering. "I've asked myself the same question. Maybe I didn't want to call attention to myself. I get enough of that in Erin just for being the child of my parents. I should have gone away to school to begin with."

"I'm surprised your father didn't tell you to file a complaint under Title IX."

"I didn't know about it until recently." The tone of Marvin's voice would have frozen saltwater in Hawaii.

"It's not as if I had the worst of it," Zoe snapped at him.

"What do you mean?" Banfield pounced.

"I mean there was another girl there at the time, an administrative assistant, and he helped himself to her boobs when her hands were otherwise occupied."

Judging by the stunned look on his face, this was brand-new intel to Marvin Slade, county prosecutor. For McCabe & Co.—or maybe I should say Banfield & Co.—this was just what we'd been hoping for: a line on another victim with a bigger axe to grind. Make that "survivor."

"Are you sure?" Banfield pressed.

"I used my phone to record him doing it, but the survivor didn't want to come forward publicly."

"What!" I think that was me.

"I guess Burch thought she was easy pickings because of her history," Zoe said. "She was in her twenties, not a student. It was common knowledge in the hallways that she'd 'been around'"—air quotes—"before somebody at SBU got her an admin job in the business school. I think she practically had her own suite in the Erin jail. Maybe that's why Burch thought he could go further with her and get by with it.

"Anyway, when she told me he was handling the merchandise, I decided to catch him at it. I just made sure I was nearby whenever Burch maneuvered it so the two of them were off in a corner by themselves. It took a couple of weeks, but I finally got some clear video of the old guy getting handy."

Marvin found his voice, and it wasn't a quiet one: "That's sexual imposition. You had a legal responsibility to report it. Haven't I taught you anything?"

Zoe had her mouth open for a snappy response to that, but Erica intervened. "Failure to report a felony is a crime, but sexual imposition is not a felony in Ohio. It's a third-degree misdemeanor under Section 2907.06 of the Ohio Revised Code."

"You must be an expert in that particular section," Marvin snapped, "since you've defended a number of violators of it."

"I don't choose my clients," Erica shot back. "They choose me. And everybody's entitled to a defense. And by the way, did you ever notice that juries of their peers found some of those clients charged under that statute innocent?"

"Stop it!" Zoe yelled. *Who's the parent here?* "Both of you! It wasn't my story to tell. I tried to get the survivor to file a complaint, but she wouldn't."

"You know as well as I do, Marvin, there's a good reason these cases are usually settled out of court." Erica looked at the rest of us, in case we didn't know as well as she and Marvin did. "Testifying in court about harassment or abuse can be traumatizing for survivors. Suppose Zoe had taken the video to law enforcement and Marvin indicted Burch. If Burch didn't agree to a plea deal, Zoe could have been dragged into court as a witness on the sexual imposition. And that means that, inevitably, she would have had to testify about her own experience with Burch. And Burch's attorney wouldn't have been gentle."

"You should know," Marvin muttered. Erica talked over to him.

"Zoe's a tough young woman"—said with pride—"but a half-day in court being interrogated by Evan Farleigh might have affected her for years. Trust me on that. No mother would want that for her daughter."

This declaration meant something to Marvin Slade. He telegraphed that with the widening of his eyes. I just had no idea what. Maybe it had something to do with realizing that Mama Bear had been in the know all along and he'd been shut out. Or maybe not.

Whatever it was, I don't think Mac missed it. He gave his beard a workover as Banfield riposted.

"Granting all of that," she said in a carefully neutral tone, "surely you can see that the murder has changed everything, Zoe."

"But the survivor had nothing to do with the murder!"

"You can't know that," her father told her. "You need to tell us who she is and turn over the video."

"I won't!" I had a sudden vision of Zoe in boxing gloves. "And you can't make me. Look, the girl he grabbed has already had enough to do with cops and courts to last her a lifetime. Besides, Burch knew what I had. He left both of us alone after that. She stuck with the job for a few months after I transferred to Miami in the Spring Semester of 2017."

Sounds like blackmail to me, but I won't tell if you won't.

"Whatever you think," Banfield said, "it's not at all far-fetched that Burch's killer is somebody he took advantage of." She paused, probably girding her metaphorical loins. "Or a parent of such a person."

"I can get that," Erica said with gusto. "I wanted to punch Burch in his nether regions myself."

With gloves off, I bet.

"That's only human," her ex allowed. *How would you know, Marv?* "But justice is not a DIY project. That's why we have laws and courts and prisons. When a crime is committed, it isn't just the injured party who is harmed but the whole community. That's why only the state can be the agent of justice."

You know, that actually makes sense.

"Well said!"

But Marvin looked too disconcerted to enjoy Mac's praise. "This entire conversation puts me in an awkward position as prosecutor."

"Well, it's above my paygrade," Banfield said. "All I know is that I'd really like to talk to anybody who's happy to see Warren Burch dead."

"Try his students," Zoe said. "I hear his tests were really tough."

Chapter Sixteen
Bad Business?

"Good thing Zoe has a good lawyer," I said after we escaped from the Slade lovefest. "She's sitting on evidence of a crime."

"But only a misdemeanor," Banfield said. "You heard Erica. But why the hell is touching a person's body parts without permission only a misdemeanor, anyway?" Her normally cheerful demeanor was notable by its absence.

We were in the cruiser, heading toward Court Street and a conference with Gibbons at the police station to compare notes.

"Perhaps that is a question to ask your state legislator," Mac said, wisely dodging the issue. He switched gears. "As a father myself, I certainly do not envy Marvin's position. He is in a pickle, torn between filial affection and the demands of the law."

"He's a politician," I said. "He'll figure it out and still sleep at night."

Banfield waxed even less sympathetic. "I don't care whether Mr. Slade sleeps or not. This fourth woman is a promising suspect. She has a record and a reason to hate Burch. We need to get her name."

"The more you and Marvin pressed Miss Slade on that point, the more obdurate she became," Mac reminded us unnecessarily.

"Why would the fourth woman"—I like that phrase; it reminded me of *The Third Man*—"kill Burch now? She worked for Burch at the same time as Zoe, so that was two years ago."

"Maybe she just saw him again on campus and her anger boiled over," Banfield said. She wasn't letting this theory get away easily.

"But she isn't on campus anymore," I objected.

"Of that we cannot be sure," Mac said thoughtfully. "All we know is that the fourth woman left the employment of Dean Burch 'a few months after' Zoe transferred out of SBU. Perhaps she works in some other department at the university."

"Maybe we need a timetable on all this."

"Excellent idea, Jefferson. I shall prepare one."

"Well, at least this other woman unnamed by Zoe knows her way around Mackie Hall."

"Maybe some of Burch's business partners did, too," Banfield said, showing an open mind as to suspects. "After all, it's a business school. We'll see what Jack's turned up."

"Not too promising," Lt. Col. L. Jack Gibbons reported. Banfield hung on his every word, even though there were only three of them.

While we talked to the three students over the past two days, Gibbons interviewed the majority owners of a high-end gift shop (A Touch of Glass), a wine store (Wine Not), a dog-training school (Canine College), a vape shop (Vaporize), a tuxedo and gown rental (Black & White), and a new alternative funeral establishment specializing in natural or "green" burials (Dust to Dust). Those were the businesses Catherine Burch had named as being her husband's local investments. I figured Oscar was keeping the vape place in business all by himself.

"They all told the same story," Gibbons said. "Burch provided modest amounts of start-up money for ventures he liked in return for a small ownership position. But he wasn't in it for the long haul. When a business he invested in flourished, he took his money back along with a nice profit. A Touch of Glass, for instance. Clarice Stanfield at said he already liquidated his position in her store."

"In other words," I said, "he was a small-scale venture capitalist."

"If you say so. Of course, these investments didn't always go well. Black & White is having a going-out-of-business sale right now." *Maybe I can get a good deal on a tux. I've always wanted to own a tux.*

"Why don't his business partners make good suspects?" Banfield asked.

Gibbons gave her his full attention. *Very* full attention, I noticed. "Because they aren't his business partners. Well, they are but they aren't. His ownership share was very small in each case, and he had nothing to do with running the business. So, none of the majority owners insured Burch's life. At least, they said they didn't, and they'd be stupid to lie about it."

"What if Burch demanded his money back from one of those entrepreneurs right away and he or she couldn't give it to him without upending the business?" I said. "That would be a dandy motive for murder."

"That hardly seems likely, Jefferson." *Wet blanket.* "What investor as astute as Warren Burch would put at risk money that he could not afford to lose?"

"I'll circle back to his wife anyway and see if he had a sudden need of cash," Gibbons said. He made a note. *Good man.*

"Did any of the business owners have a connection to the business school?" Banfield asked him.

"Not that they would admit to. Nothing recent, anyway—a couple of them are grads of the school or of the university. I have another idea about a suspect with an SBU connection, though. None of you are going to like it."

Mac cocked an eyebrow. Banfield sat forward. I just felt dread.

"There's a name that kept coming up in Burch's smartphone calendar: Grant Kingsley."

I let out my breath. "Oh, well, that's an easy one. Burch was on the board of the Altiora Corp. at GK's suggestion. GK told me that. Burch was even on the audit committee."

Why did the normally bland Gibbons look so triumphant?

"Exactly. Isn't the head of the audit committee just the person who would know of any financial shenanigans on the corporate books—like maybe embezzling by the senior vice president, Grant Kingsley?"

Chapter Seventeen
The Three Students

"Ingenious theory, you must admit, Jefferson," Mac said on the way back to campus.

"I'm not in the mood to admit anything."

"Grant has always been very supportive of me," Banfield volunteered.

Grant? I wish this woman were a fictional character, and that I created her.

"You know our interim president, then?" I said.

She nodded. "He was Air Force, you know. We met at a wounded warrior event, and a few times since."

"Well, that won't hurt."

"Hurt what?"

"Has it not occurred to you, Aurelia, that we are in the awkward position of interviewing our temporary superior in the context of a murder investigation?" Mac said.

"It'll be fine."

"We don't actually have to tell him Gibbons is giving him the hairy eyeball, do we?" I asked.

"Really, it'll be fine."

As (good) luck would have it, I already had an appointment that day to meet GK outside the offices of WIJC, our campus radio station. Tony Lampwicke, a long-time SBU employee, was going to record an interview for the weekly *Crosscurrents* program. Given GK's deep interest in the investigation, it was only natural that Mac and Banfield came along to give him an update. At least, I hoped that's what he would think.

We were early for the WIJC appointment, but GK was earlier. We found him pacing in front of the glassed-in offices of the station, wearing an expensive-looking black alpaca overcoat.

He didn't need any introductions.

"Aurelia!" he said. "Good to see you." He gave her a handshake and a quick, one-armed hug. "And you're Sebastian McCabe! People call you Mac, don't they?" *Most people.* GK eyed the crutches. "What happened to your—"

"A mere trifle," I assured him.

"Well, it's a pleasure to meet you, Mac. I have a standing order at Mo's Mysteries & Marvels for all your books as they roll out. I'm Damon Devlin's biggest fan."

Not while Sebastian McCabe is alive, you're not.

"I am honored." Mac preened, tried to look modest (not his best trick), accepted a Cuban cigar from GK, and made the cigar disappear by sleight of hand all within the space of maybe thirty seconds. Good thing he moved fast, because GK was ready for business. He didn't spare the hokey magic trick more than a passing chuckle.

"What can you tell me about the murder?" he asked. "I'm sure Tony won't mind if I'm a few minutes late."

I'm sure. Tony Lampwicke uses bigger words than Mac, and more of them, wrapped up in a cultivated Oxford English accent. He's from Hamilton, Ohio, about eighty miles up the road from Erin.

"We've been busy," I assured him. "So has Gibbons of the Erin police."

"Good."

Not entirely.

"Maybe we'd better go someplace we can talk."

We found a deserted hallway with a small table and enough chairs, although Mac was squeezed. GK sat across from Banfield, with Mac and me on either side of him. Banfield gave him the lowdown:

"Between the Erin police and us, we talked with his wife, an antagonist on the business faculty, three students with whom he behaved inappropriately, and six local business owners with whom he had invested." That didn't count Saylor-Mackie, who had an alibi tighter than a hatband.

"And?"

"I wouldn't say we have a suspect or even a person of interest."

She elaborated, giving him a brief and factual account of our efforts over the past two days. We had covered a lot of territory without uncovering much.

GK frowned. "At least it's a good thing that none of our former students seems likely to be the killer. That would be terrible publicity."

You could say that.

"But Lieutenant Colonel Gibbons did have an interesting idea that I wanted to bounce off of you," Banfield said. *Interesting is one word for it.* "We've been looking at Burch as a former dean and as an investor in a number of local businesses, but he was more than that. He was also a member of the Altiora Corp. board and chair of its audit committee."

She paused. GK's face said, "*Tell me something I don't know.*"

"So, Gibbons wondered whether the head of a company's audit committee might uncover financial irregularities"—*that sounds much better than "shenanigans"*— "in the corporate books."

"He'd better!" GK held up his hands. "I mean, that's why the audit committee is there."

"Then wouldn't that be a strong murder motive?"

"Sure!" He turned to his right. "You could use that, Mac." Back to Banfield: "But in real life the chair of the audit committee isn't the only one who would know about any problems. There's a committee, and the committee oversees the work of auditors. It's not possible that one person would be the only one to know."

There went GK's highly hypothetical motive for homicide. I almost fainted with relief.

"Well, then," Mac said, "I would certainly not use that in a Damon Devlin story. I strive for verisimilitude." *Since when?* "From what Jefferson tells me, you seem to have known Warren Burch rather well. He recruited you as an adjunct instructor when he was dean, and you in turn recommended him for the Altiora board."

"That's right. We weren't golfing buddies, but I respected his business acumen. I was shocked when I learned from the *Observer* about his behavior toward female subordinates. I never dreamed he was that sort of man. In the Air Force, he'd have been busted a rank and retired. At least, I hope so."

Banfield looked skeptical.

"When was the last time you saw him?" Mac asked.

"We went to breakfast—let me think. It was a week ago Wednesday. I'd been trying to get together with him for weeks."

"What for?"

"To suggest that it might be best if he resign from the board in view of the revelations about the whole reason for his departure from the deanship."

"How did he react to that suggestion?"

"Very poorly. He didn't even finish his waffles."

Mac looked horrified. "He must have been quite upset."

"I'll say. He was pissed at me, at the *Observer*, at the university, at the young ladies who turned him in, and at the low quality of students today. He left in a huff, so it hit me all the harder when I learned on the road Wednesday that he'd been killed."

"On the road?" I echoed.

He nodded. "I was at corporate headquarters in Connecticut from Monday until I flew back on Wednesday afternoon for the board meeting. Confidentially, Father Joe tipped me over the weekend that he was thinking of resigning, and I was clearing the decks with my bosses at the home office so I could deal with that."

Mac raised an eyebrow. I didn't need a tree to fall on me: Grant Kingsley had an iron-clad alibi for the late-night murder of Warren Burch. How convenient of him to supply it without being asked.

Mac went outside to smoke the Cuban cigar (magically reappeared!) and Banfield went back to her office to brief Ed Decker. That left me with GK and Tony Lampwicke. The *Crosscurrents* interview ("What is your favorite British novel?") was about as much fun as cleaning out my sock drawer, but GK acquitted himself well ("*Brideshead Revisited.*") The ordeal had just begun when Banfield sent Mac and me a text: *"Will have Jack check & make sure Grant was in Connecticut the night of the murder."* Mac sent her back a thumbs up sign.

I was impressed with Banfield's savvy on that, presuming she just wasn't looking for a reason to interface with "Jack." But half my mind was on Warren Burch's funeral visitation, which was coming up that night. I hate wakes, but I'd agreed to give Mac a lift to the obsequies.

Several hours later, therefore, I arrived at the house on Half Moon Street and found Mac in his study, i.e., man cave. Hard at work on the computer, he hadn't even tapped himself a beer.

"Warren Burch's survivors are an impressive trio of young women, Jefferson," he commented without looking up.

"You're still thinking about them?"

"I have compiled a timetable of their interactions with the deceased."

"Why?"

"Desperation, old boy."

He printed it out and handed it to me:

THE THREE STUDENTS
A Chronology

Amal Abood   *Work-study: Spring 2015*
Asked to: adjust air vent, pick up
books, try on T-shirt
Transferred: Fall 2015

Zoe Slade   *Student intern: Fall 2015*
Asked to: bend over
Burch looked down her blouse,
commented on posterior
Transferred: Spring 2016

Madison Lee   *Student intern: Spring 2016*
Asked to: reach high bookcases,
give dancing lessons
Burch called her "honey"
Graduated: December 2016
Filed complaint January 2017

Spring and fall referred to semesters rather than seasons. At St. Benignus, the spring semester begins in late January and ends with final exams and commencement in May. The fall semester begins in late August and ends with finals and commencement in December. There are also short winter and summer terms. Burch's settlement allowed him to sit out the 2017–18 academic year and return as a professor for the fall semester of 2018–19, which was just wrapping up.

"Okay, so what does this chronology tell you?" I asked.

"Not a confounded thing, blast it!"

And yet, that piece of paper eventually was to provide the convoluted McCabe brain with a key clue.

"The fourth woman had a much bigger axe to grind against Burch than the former students we interviewed," I pointed out. "Stuff like making the students bend over or stand on a chair to adjust the air vent, even looking down Ms. Slade's blouse, wasn't quite in the same league as getting grabby. Too bad we don't know anything about her."

"On the contrary, we know quite a bit about that young lady."

"Like what?"

"We know the following facts." He ticked them off on his fingers. "She was not a student. She is older than Zoe Slade. She has spent time in Oscar's lockup, which indicates a police record. She worked in the dean's office at the same time as Zoe Slade. She no longer works there."

Five facts, five fingers. A handful!

"I see what you mean. With all that to go on, we should be able to find her name in the records of the dean's office on Monday morning." It turned out that wasn't necessary. But I record this so that you know we would have identified her even without the gift that came our way later that night. "As you pointed out, she might still work on campus. If so, she would have motive and opportunity. Wouldn't that make her the perfect suspect?"

"Almost. There is one more attribute necessary for perfection in that regard."

"What's that?"

"Invisibility to security cameras."

Chapter Eighteen
Friends May Call

"For an unpopular fellow, Professor Burch certainly attracted a full complement of mourners," Mac observed, looking around at the packed crowd for the visitation that evening.

"Who says they're all mourning?"

It occurred to me, maybe unworthily, that the SBU teachers and administrators among those at Hawes & Holder Funeral Home that evening may have just been trying to fill up an unexpected hole in their calendars. GK had canceled the annual faculty-staff Christmas party in deference to the departed.

Dust to Dust, the green burial company that was among the local start-ups in which Burch invested, apparently hadn't hurt Hawes & Holder's trade any. The place was booming. Warren Burch occupied one visitation room and Mallory Lambert in the other. Tall and lean Jonathan Hawes, husband to Mo Russert[5] of Mo's Mysteries & Marvels, supplied warmth and sympathy. He once portrayed Sherlock Holmes in Mac's play, *1895*, and he looked the part.

"How's business?" I asked.

People are just dying to get in here, Jeff.

"Our second home is as busy as this one."

"Not much competition from green burials, eh?"

---

[5] The events surrounding their wedding in Barbados remain to be chronicled, possibly under the title *A Destination Murder*.

As I understand it, going green for the final sendoff means no toxic embalming fluids, concrete vaults, or metal caskets. Bodies are just cloaked in biodegradable material and buried.

"That will always be a niche market," Jonathan opined.

Mac and I were there to pay our respects to a departed colleague. We'd talked it over and decided we owed Burch that, even though the presence of anybody from SBU would probably make Catherine Burch and her husband's haters equally unhappy. But I'm not sure it even sunk in to Mrs. Burch that we were there, along with Father Joe, Grant Kingsley, Lesley Saylor-Mackie, Dante Peter O'Neill of SBU's School of Arts and Humanities, and Wendy Yazane of the business school. The widow shook our hands and mumbled a few words, as protocol demanded, but she appeared medicated.

Duty done, we didn't leave right away. Wakes are always a good chance to catch up with acquaintances you haven't seen in a while.

"That's Burch's lawyer over there, Evan Farleigh," I told Mac after a few minutes of mingling.

"He is the one who looks like a lion wearing glasses, is he not?"

"Yeah, that's him, the big mane of yellow hair. That young man he's in such earnest conversation with is Jason Danvers."

"Ah, yes, Warren's most vociferous defender."

"Possibly excluding Farleigh and Mrs. Burch, but only possibly."

"Hello, Cody, McCabe."

This was a voice out of the past, and not such a happy past. In his years as provost and academic vice president of St. Benignus, Ralph Pendergast regarded Mac as a menace and me as an obstacle. Just one big dysfunctional family! But we had warmed up to each other now that Ralph labored as president of the Sussex County Convention & Visitors Bureau and no longer poked his sharp nose into my office.

"I'm sorry that Father Pirelli is leaving office under such unfortunate circumstances," he said. "He's a good man and deserved better." Was that moisture I saw in the eyes behind his rimless glasses? Probably not, but you never know. Ralph was all numbers by day, but at night he liked to let down his slicked back hair (metaphorically) and listen to jazz. One of his current initiatives at the Visitors Bureau was an effort to bring a summer jazz festival to town. More immediately—the next day, in fact—was a new event called Santafest that Ralph dreamed up to keep downtown hopping the week after Small Business Saturday. Ralph's Grinch days were behind him!

"A good man indeed," Mac echoed Ralph.

"Nobody would disagree with that," I threw in.

"Finances were not his forte," Ralph said, a reflective look on his face. "But I have come to believe that he is, nonetheless, the heart and soul of the institution."

Maybe that *was* a tear or two I spotted.

"However," he moved on, "I know that Grant Kingsley will serve admirably in the interim."

No doubt Ralph knew whereof he spoke, having hobnobbed a lot with the trustees when he was at SBU.

"Did you know the deceased well?" Mac rumbled.

"Apparently not as well as I thought." Ralph lowered his voice, not that anybody in that crowd was eavesdropping. They all had their own conversations going. "I was involved in his appointment as dean, of course. His misconduct in that office shocked and appalled me." He paused. "I'm really here for Catherine. Funerals are for the living. She must have been terribly hurt by all the bad press about Warren, and now this." He shook that off. "Give me a call someday, Cody. I have a few ideas about promoting SBU's Bijou productions. There should be a sizeable regional audience for quality theater. Perhaps we can do lunch."

With a nod, he was off and soon in the company of Fred Gaffe, author of the "Old Gaffer" column in the *Observer*. Fred never misses a wake. He calls it research.

"Life is strange," I mused as I followed Ralph 2.0 with my eyes.

"And wonderful," Mac added.

He didn't move much because of his bum leg and the crutches, but people came up to him. Evan Farleigh, for example, glad-handed us just to show there was no hard feelings about my indiscretion to Maggie Barton. Maybe he figured that Burch was over it, so he might as well be, too.

Inevitably, though, there was some discussion of the guest of honor at the wake.

"He was my friend as well as my client," Farleigh offered. He really *did* look like a lion in glasses. Now that Mac had put that image in my head, I'd never get it back out again. Farleigh was also big, and not especially well-tailored. His belly flopped over his belt.

"Do you have any idea who killed him?" Mac asked.

"I don't think I should speculate. I might wind up naming somebody I have to defend in court!"

I think he was kidding, if only because Farleigh & Farleigh didn't do much criminal defense work. It was mostly a civil practice, although he'd spiced that up a little lately with the occasional drug case (of which there was no lack). The firm was named for father and son. The father died years ago, but Evan kept the double name until his daughter passed the bar and joined him in the outfit.

"I will say this," he added. "More than a few of Warren's friends and admirers think he would be alive today if St. Benignus hadn't allowed his name to be dragged through the mud. No offense, gentlemen."

None taken, asshole. I guess he wasn't over it after all.

"That would imply you believe his murder was in some way connected with his regrettable actions," Mac observed.

"You should be a lawyer."

What, and give up fiction?

"Do you have any concrete reason for such a belief?" Mac pressed.

"No. And I told you I won't speculate. I'm just telling you what people are telling me."

He drifted away. *And good riddance!*

Within a few minutes we tried to make our own escape and move to the Mallory Lambert visitation in the other parlor, but Mac's progress on his crutches through the crowded hallway serving both visitations was slow.

"Aren't you Sebastian McCabe?"

Why doesn't anybody ever say, "Aren't you Jeff Cody, author of all those griping true-crime books about What's-His-Name?"

The questioner was an attractive woman in her late forties, with somewhat disheveled auburn hair and green eyes. She wore black slacks, a gray silk blouse, and a string of pearls. I wasn't surprised to find out later she'd been a college volleyball player. She looked vaguely familiar.

Mac admitted to being Sebastian McCabe.

"I'm Helen Calloway." She thrust out her hand, wasting no time about it. "Team physician for the Lady Dragons."

That's where I'd see her before—on the basketball court! It had been some time since I'd caught a game. I should do that more often. Sports are important for small schools like ours. They help boost enrollment, which is critical to the bottom line. Having spent some time shooting hoops myself, the Lady Dragons are my favorite of our teams.

"And you must be Jeff Cody." *Finally!*

She shook my hand, too, in a businesslike way.

"I see you all the time on campus," she told Mac. "You must be tired of people telling you how much they love your books."

He coughed modesty. "In all candor, Dr. Calloway, one never tires of hearing that." *At least this "one" doesn't.*

"I picked up an e-copy of *Now You See It* a few weeks back on sale. Running into you reminds me I need to read it." *Ouch! On sale and unread!* No wonder Mac flinched. "Say, you look like you're in pain."

Mac looked ruefully at his still-bandaged ankle. "I never knew a sprain could be so excruciating. Ibuprofen has not been as effective as I would have hoped."

"I could prescribe you something stronger. I'm pretty sure oxycodone would take care of it."

Just what the world needs—Sebastian McCabe on drugs. But I didn't think he'd go that far to emulate Sherlock Holmes. In addition to being a great painkiller, oxycodone is classed by the U.S. Drug Enforcement Administration as a Schedule II narcotic. That means it carries a high potential for abuse and is considered dangerous. (I looked that up.)

"Isn't that how a lot of people get addicted these days—prescription medications?" a new voice asked before Mac could respond. Maggie Barton looked every inch of her seventy-some years, with her broad shoulders sagging and her pink hair drooping. She must have just stepped out of the visitation for her great-niece, Mallory Lambert, in the adjacent room.

"There is some risk." Helen Calloway's tone was cool. Maybe she didn't develop a good bedside manner working with self-confident female athletes who towered over her. "But that can be exaggerated. It's easy to forget that opioids have relieved the suffering of a lot people."

By killing them. Even as I thought that, with Mallory in mind, I realized the doctor was right. That was the other side of the story, which Tall Rawls had addressed in the *Observer*. There was even a series of "Don't Punish Pain" rallies that summer to advocate for the availability of opioids for extreme pain sufferers.

Calloway turned back to Mac. "It was a pleasure to meet you, Professor. Perhaps we can get together for lunch on campus some time."

Who knew that a funeral home was such a great place to catch lunch invitations?

Mac belatedly thanked her for her kind offer of pain relief and allowed as how he would soldier on.

With a couple more nods and murmurs, she was gone.

"Who was that?" Maggie asked in her wake.

"Dr. Calloway," I said. "The team doctor for the Lady Dragons." Maggie looked thoughtful.

"We wanted to pay our respects to your nephew," Mac told her.

"I'll introduce you. I was just going to call Uber for a ride home. I don't feel well. This trauma with Mallory has taken its toll on me."

"You don't drive anymore?" I said.

She shook her head. "Not at night. I can't see well enough."

Even by day Maggie Barton was a menace on the road. "You don't have to call Uber. We'll give you ride." It would be a tight squeeze in the Volkswagen, but doable.

"Thanks, Jeff. I'd appreciate it."

Maggie took us into the other parlor, where we briefly met and sympathized with a dazed Barry Lambert and his wife, Sally. They had three other children. When I had my first kidney stone, Dr. LaBelle asked me to rate the pain on a scale of 1 to 10, but the agony of having a child die must be somewhere off that scale. And today it seems that can happen to anybody. I wished Lynda and I hadn't made plans for that evening. I just wanted to stay home and hug our kids.

On the way out of the funeral home, with Maggie in tow, I happened to notice Evan Farleigh in a small side room near the entrance. He took a pill out of his pocket and handed it to a powerfully built man with thinning straw hair. I yanked on Mac's sleeve.

"Well, have you solved it yet?" Maggie asked before he could turn in my direction. "Burch's murder, I mean."

"When I do, you shall be among the first to know," Mac assured her.

"All right, you haven't solved it, then. Who do you suspect?"

Whom!

"Oh, come on, Maggie!" That was me. "You know better than that."

She giggled. "You can't blame an old gal for trying. I'd love to score a beat on Johanna just to prove I can still do it. We have this little in-house competition going. And, heck, who knows? This could be my swan song."

"How so?" Mac asked.

By this time we were at my car. Maggie eyed it skeptically before remembering to answer. Okay, it's small. But it's roomy.

"I'm thinking that with Father Joe leaving SBU, this might be a good time for me to hang it up, too," she explained. "I don't need the money and I'm running out of energy."

Not so long ago I'd been daydreaming of Maggie's retirement, but now the idea took me aback. It seemed that the speed of change in my little world was accelerating.

Just then, Mac and I both got pinged. I pulled out my smartphone first. It was a text to both of us from Banfield: *jack can't find record of gk flying out of town this week*

So much for his volunteered alibi.

Chapter Nineteen
Darts

"Sounds like you and Mac had a busy day sleuthing," said Sister Mary Margaret Malone, AKA Triple M (to me) or Sister Polly. "Popcorn must be exhausted."

"Nobody likes a sarcastic sister," I informed her. "Besides, Popcorn's happy that I'm not a micromanager."

"Children, please," Lynda said as she lifted her first Manhattan of the evening. "No fighting in public."

She looked fabulous in a dashing red beret, somewhat overdressed for our outing at Bobbie McGee's Sports Bar. Her long earrings matched the color of the headgear, but her fingernails were painted alternately red and green in the Christmas spirit. Mac and Kate were watching the Cody offspring for a few hours. Kate kept texting pictures.

To my utter surprise, Gibbons and Banfield were also at Bobbie's—playing darts! Gibbons seemed to be ahead. Shouldn't an archer like Banfield be good at darts? Her long brown hair, liberated in an off-duty pony tail, swung vigorously as she threw. She also wore distinctively down-time silver earrings, large and round. Gibbons had his shirt sleeves rolled up, showing off impressive muscular development. I could imagine those two throwing axes if the trend ever hit Erin.

"Their liaising," I told my tablemates.

"Is that what you call it?" Triple M waggled her eyebrows. Remember, she was in the army before she was in the convent. Her short dark hair, parted in the middle, could even be a military cut.

"Their body language says the relationship isn't just professional, but also isn't very far advanced," Lynda judged. "I'd say they're jogging happily to first base together."

How do women know this stuff? And since when does my wife use sports analogies to talk about romance?

"She must like the strong, silent type," Triple M offered. She knows Gibbons. Nobody is stronger or more silent than L. Jack.

While this idle speculation of a possible cross-agency romance continued, the Cody brain was stuck back on that text from Banfield earlier. She said Gibbons couldn't confirm Grant Kingsley's story of being at the home office when Burch was murdered. That gave some substance to Gibbons's suspicions of GK in the face of Banfield's skepticism. Would that impress her or peeve her? Hard to tell. I didn't know her well enough to say. But I'd never seen Gibbons roll up his shirt sleeves before, so something was going on there. Clearly, this wasn't the time and place to ask him for more details about GK's non-alibi. And since Mac only responded with a grunt when he saw Banfield's message, I had to process this myself.

WWMD—What would Mac do? He would list the possible explanations. I mentally did so while zoning out on the Lynda-Triple M gabfest:

(a) *Gibbons messed up.* Impossible. Not even on the table. Nobody is infallible, but he wouldn't make a mistake involving an electronic "paper trail."

(b) *GK lied.* Why would he lie? Only one awful reason. I had visions of a headline blaring **SBU INTERIM PRESIDENT ARRESTED IN PROF'S DEATH**. That would never do.

(c)

There must be a "c." Maybe I would have come up with one if half my brain hadn't been struggling to remember what I wanted to tell Mac, something I saw—

"Johanna is a little upset at the way Maggie has taken over the story," Lynda said. "Crime is supposed to be her beat."

"Yeah, well, SBU is Maggie's beat," I countered. "And she sure has been aggressive with it in this case. No pre-retirement letdown for her."

"So, who does Mac think killed Warren Burch?" Triple M said. The Banfield-Gibbons topic apparently had been exhausted in my mental absence.

How should I know? I responded with a non-answer:

"We're paying a lot of attention to the survivors of Burch's unwanted attentions and their family members. Gibbons is going down other paths." I wasn't going to elaborate on those paths, even though I knew both my companions could give the Sphynx lessons in discretion. Their ears weren't the only ones in the place.

"I guess you have to start someplace," Triple M said, "but is it really plausible that somebody killed him for what he did back when he was dean?"

"Sometimes the effects of abuse grow over time," Lynda said.

"Well, yes, that's true."

"We've interviewed all three women who talked to the dean of students and the director of human resources about Burch," I reported, "but there's another survivor that he groped. That's illegal and more serious than what he did to the others. We know there's a video of the touching—it's on a smartphone—but we can't get access to it. Never mind why. So, we'd like to talk to this fourth woman. She wasn't a student, but she worked for Burch. Apparently, she'd had some trouble with the law, not a model citizen, which may make her reluctant to cooperate. We don't know her name at this point, but we should be able to find out from business school records."

Triple M all but gasped before I'd even finished talking. "But she didn't—she wouldn't—"

Words failed her. Lynda put down her Manhattan and held Triple M's hand. I wouldn't say she looked at me like I was a brute, but I don't think she harbored any great desire for my husbandly attentions at that point. Nor was that foremost on my mind, for a rare change. I was busy having a flash of inspiration.

"You got that woman her job in the dean's office!" I said. I have not hung around Sebastian McCabe more than twenty years for nothing. As campus minister by trade and volunteer jailhouse chaplain in her spare time, what could be more natural for Triple M than bridging the two worlds by getting an inmate a job on campus?

"It seemed a good idea at the time," the good sister said miserably. "She was trying to start over. And she made it. She's been working steadily and taking a class when she can fit it in."

A model citizen!

A big shout went up from the crowd watching the dart action. Somebody had just scored a bullseye.

"Well, don't just stop there!" I said. "What's her name?"

Triple M shook her head. "I can't tell you that. I tried to get her to make a complaint when it happened, but she wouldn't. Maybe she'll talk to you guys and Mac, no cops involved, just so you can cross her off the suspect list."

"Why us?" Lynda asked.

"Because you're sort of old friends of hers."

Chapter Twenty
The Fourth Woman

"Can't I have a cigarette, Sister Polly? I need a cigarette."

"You have my deepest sympathy," Mac intoned gloomily.

"Offer it up for the poor souls in Purgatory," Triple M advised 28-year-old Minnie Cooper.

"I call them my homies," Minnie volleyed back.

It was Saturday morning in the campus ministry office, and the beneficiary of these variant smoking-related messages was the fourth woman. Calling Lynda and me her "old friends" was a bit of a stretch on Triple M's part. We first met Cooper exactly six years earlier, when she was doing community service[6]. She had cut her long brown hair since then and dyed it in the trendy "toasted coconut" color. At least, that's what Lynda called it when I described it. Lynda wasn't with us, and (as promised) neither were the official gendarmes.

Mac tried to get this train back on the rails.

He leaned forward on one of his crutches. "We are interested in your interactions with the late Warren Burch," he told our guest—as if she didn't know.

"The old goat palmed my pomegranates."

Mac arched an eyebrow.

"You know, groped my guavas."

---

[6] See "Santa Crime" in *Rogues Gallery* (MX Publishing, 2014).

I don't know why Triple M looked so mortified at this rather delicate description of what Ohio Revised Code Section 2907.06 considers "sexual imposition." I'd expected a more graphic account.

"He didn't make so free with Zoe," Cooper amplified. "She's a good girl and her parents are lawyers. I'm not a good girl. I came with a rep when Sr. Polly got me the job. Burch wasn't just being nice when he agreed to hire me. He knew what he was getting."

Her bravado tone struck me as a pose. The offenses that landed Cooper in Oscar's lockup were minor offences, mostly a matter of sticky fingers with the occasional disturbing the peace. She liked jewelry that didn't belong to her.

"Our understanding is that Dean Burch touched you more than once, and that Zoe Slade recorded an instance of it on her phone," Mac said. In court that might have been called a leading question, but nobody objected.

"Yeah, that's right. She showed it to Burch. He left me alone after that, until Zoe transferred out. Then he started in on me again."

"And how did you react?"

"After the second or third time he didn't pay attention when I said 'hands off,' I kneed him in his nuts." *The Erica Slade School of Conflict Resolution!* Cooper looked at Triple M. "I didn't tell you this before, but I did that because of you, Sister."

"Me?" Sister Mary Margaret Malone, campus minister, looked horrified. "What did I do?"

"You treated me like a human being, that's what. You got me that job, which should have been a really good job, and you gave me some self-respect. That's why I pushed back on him." *That's one way of putting it.*

"Oh, Minnie!" They hugged.

After a suitable interval, Mac said: "And then?"

"Then he fired me. I wouldn't have minded so much, except that Sister Polly got me the job and I felt like I let her down. Burch threatened to accuse me of stealing exam questions if I reported him. He still taught one class a year then. If he did that, I knew nobody would believe me."

"But there was the video!" I said.

"I didn't want to drag Zoe into it."

"Most admirable," Mac said.

Triple M disagreed. "No, it's not. This isn't just about Minnie and Zoe and whoever else was hurt directly. There's a justice issue here, Mac. I told Minnie at the time that law enforcement should be notified."

"That obligation has been obviated by Professor Burch's demise."

"I can't say I'm sorry," the fourth woman declared. "When the crap about Burch and the other three women hit the fan in the newspaper, I was afraid somebody would get my name from Zoe. I'm glad it was you guys. You were okay to me last time. Maybe I can stay out of it as far as anybody else goes. I mean, Burch is dead, like Mac said, so what difference does it make now?"

"Minnie's afraid that if her name gets dragged into this, even as an innocent party, her ancient dirty laundry might get aired and it will hurt her," Triple M. said. "She wants to leave the past behind."

Motive! I thought. *In a strange way, Minnie Cooper benefits from the murder.*

"I've been keeping my nose clean," Cooper said. Said nose had a ring in it. "I haven't even been to the new jail. How is it?"

"Just like home," I assured her.

Triple M glared at me, but she's too nice to do it well.

"I don't want to lose my job," Cooper added. "It's a good one."

"Do you work on campus?" Mac asked.

She shook her head. "I did for a while after I left the business school, but then I got a gig at Paddles & Wheels, the boat and bike rental on Front Street. Business is booming since the bike trail along the river got extended. I love it. In the summer I get to work outside where I can get fresh air and grab a few smokes." *Somehow that seems contradictory.* "I'm taking night classes at SBU, too."

"Even more admirable," Mac opined.

"In what field?" I asked.

"Criminal justice."

Figures.

I looked at Mac. "Motive and opportunity."

"Give me a break!" Triple M cried.

"What the hell?" was the way Minnie Cooper put it.

Max explained. "I believe what Jefferson means is that you are well acquainted with the SBU campus and even had a reason for being there at night—though surely no class runs until eleven o'clock, even in the criminal justice program! And as for motive, Ms. Cooper, you yourself indicated you are relieved that Dean Burch is dead because it now seems unlikely that your name will come forward, along with your somewhat colorful history."

Triple M made a rude noise that sounded more Army than convent. "Are you guys kidding? Burch's murder is going to bring more interest to the women he molested, not less."

"Oh, crap," Cooper said.

"Ms. Banfield shall not learn your identity from us," Mac assured her. "And even if she has the happy thought of looking for another female employee in the dean's office at the same time as Zoe Slade, your name need not become public unless it is relevant to the investigation at hand."

"It's not," Triple M said sternly.

"Well, just for the record, what were you doing when Burch was killed"—*by an invisible intruder*—"around midnight Tuesday night?" I asked Cooper.

She had the grace to look sheepish. "Close your ears, Sister. I wasn't alone." If Lynda were here, she would have rolled her eyes. Triple M didn't even try to look surprised.

"And your alibi's name is?"

"A lady never tells." *Cute.* "I can get his permission to tell you if it gets to be important. But you're going to solve the murder so that I don't have to do that, McCabe. Right?"

Mac apparently thought that didn't require a reply. Instead, he said:

"And who do you think the murderer might be?"

"I'd vote for Burch's stuck-up wife. I met her in the office a couple of times throwing her weight around. She probably killed him in revenge for the humiliation when his creepiness went public."

"But she defends her husband and blames his accusers for lying," I protested. Not to mention what she said about Heidi Guildenstern.

"That's all show to cover up her embarrassment, believe me."

Mac pressed Cooper for other suspects, based on office dynamics or anything she'd seen or heard in her time in the dean's office, but that was the best she could come up with. Mac thanked her for her cooperation and wished her well in her future endeavors. She waved that away, something more important on her mind.

"I need a cigarette," she said.

"Well?" I asked Mac as we headed back to my car.

"I do not find it psychologically credible that Ms. Cooper would be so stealthy if she wished to dispatch someone."

"Me neither. Besides, I can't help liking her even though I don't want to. What about her idea that Catherine Burch did it?"

"Convoluted, but not impossible. Perhaps Mrs. Burch's apparent distress at her husband's death was artifice.

The motivation Ms. Cooper suggests, that of retribution for humiliation and embarrassment suffered by a woman of substantial social standing in the community, is plausible. Although the murder has extended that mortification by keeping the deceased's behavior in the public eye, she may not have foreseen that. Here is yet another consideration: Murder on campus instead of anywhere near her home has the obvious advantage of literally distancing Mrs. Burch from the crime. And it is certainly possible that she would know the intricacies of campus security from her husband."

So, Mac had taken the notion of Catherine Burch as a suspect seriously and thought it through. Interesting.

"Call me selfish," I said, "but the less connection there is between the killer and SBU the better I'll like it." That reminded me of the whole "Banfield says Gibbons says Grant Kingsley didn't take a plane to Connecticut" thing. Mac and I had barely discussed it before getting to Triple M's office. "Worst of all would be if our interim president killed Burch," I added.

"That would indeed be a negative development, old boy. Perhaps there is some mistake that will all be clear on Monday morning."

"We can hope. Meanwhile, Gibbons must be happy to find some support for his suspicion of GK. He doesn't usually spin theories like that."

"He did in the opera murder[7]," Mac reminded me. "This time around, however, I suspect that the good man hoped to impress Ms. Banfield."

"As if he needs to. The woman can't even say his name without drooling."

Just then, Mac's smartphone erupted into "The Ride of the Valkyries," his favorite ringtone. For a while he had it set like a telephone, but what fun is that?

---

[7] Gibbons creatively speculated that the second murder connected to the Erin Opera Company was the work of a copycat killer. See *Death Masque* (MX Publishing, 2017).

"McCabe here." His eyebrows flew up. "Oh, hello, Marvin. One o'clock? Yes, I am available. Jefferson, also? Of course. I understand. We shall see you then."

He disconnected. "The prosecutor is taking us to lunch Monday at the Nonpareil Club in Cincinnati. He says the agenda is a personal one and he requests that we keep the meeting 'on the Q.T.,' as he put it."

Chapter Twenty-One
Too Many Santas

"I'm not sure it's such a great idea to take the kids to Santafest," I told Lynda that afternoon, not for the first time. "Won't it confuse them to see all those Santas?"

As part of Ralph's latest effort to liven up the local scene, the Erin Convention & Visitors Bureau had put out an all-call on social media for amateur Santas to show up downtown in full costume. Among them would be Sebastian McCabe, who was an old hand at the role and needed no padding. He could be one of dozens or maybe even hundreds of wannabe St. Nicks answering the call on an otherwise dull Saturday.

So, how would a kid know which one to beg for a BB gun? That was my concern.

"Don't be silly, darling. You're thinking like an adult."

"I'm sorry. It won't happen again."

Lynda tugged Jake's little hat on him while I struggled with Sam. Donata was still off in her room, designing dresses or something with her crayons. "Kids know that Santa can do anything. He can squeeze his big tummy down the chimney, can't he?"

She had me there.

"Speaking of big tummies," I said, "Mac bet me that I won't be able to recognize him."

"Won't he be the one on crutches?"

"Apparently has some workaround on that, but he wouldn't say any more. Have you seen Sam's other sock?"

***

With the wind blowing off the Ohio River, Front Street was bone-chilling cold that afternoon of December 8. I envied those right jolly old elves in red, especially the ones with extra insulation in their suits. And they seemed to be everywhere. What with all the milling around as they ho-ho-hoed, I didn't try to count how many. But there were scores of them—tall and short, black and white, naturally fat and padded, and even a few bearded ladies representing the estrogen set.

Several Santas posed for selfies, mostly with adults. One strolled around playing a violin. Another stood behind a gas grill, roasting chestnuts in front of the Davenport-Lattimore Bijou Theatre. That one wore a green pin on his pointed hat, matching the one on my jacket, with an image of holly berries and the word "SHALOM" in red. Somewhat confusingly, he and his pop-up chestnut stand were just a few feet from the appropriately attired cast of *A Christmas Carol* singing (what else?) Christmas carols. Tiny Tim sat on a stadium blanket, his crutches on his lap. I didn't see the boy's face, but he was rather tall for Tiny.

Which of these Kris Kringles was Santa McCabe? Scratch the one with the violin, for sure. Not only is Mac unskilled in the playing of musical instruments (bagpipes don't qualify as such), he was currently unable to stroll. (He can sing in German, however, as you will soon see.)

"Want some candy?" Lynda's throaty whisper in my ear made me tingle to my toes. Or was that just the cold? No, it was the seductive come-on. She had me by the arm and was tugging me into the Sweet Shoppe, right next door to the theater, before you could say "double-entendre." So, I knew she meant empty calories, not another sort of sweetness. Diet or not, my beloved was in the Christmas spirit. I held Donata in the other arm, and Lynda piloted the stroller built for two. She is particularly fond of licorice hats, and the Sweet Shoppe is where in Erin to find them, along with root beer barrels, buckeyes, Bit-O-Honeys, Tootsie Rolls, Chunkys, Mary Janes, etc., all on display in big glass jars. The place is a full-employment plan for Erin's dentists!

"Help you folks?" Another Santa Claus! But this one, sans beard, was easy to identify as Wade Pennington, the latest of several generations of Penningtons dealing in such sugar-based products from Front Street. When I first met him, more than a year ago, he looked like he'd lost a lot of weight. If so, he'd gained it back. He must have recognized me, because he added, "Licorice?"

"That's a start," Lynda said—rather assertively, I thought. She lifted Donata up and let her look.

When we finally left the store all too many minutes later, I was glad the stroller had a storage compartment on the bottom so that I didn't have to carry twenty pounds (or so it seemed) of caloric confections.

But Lynda was happy, so I was happy.

Such was my mood exiting the Sweet Shoppe when a flash of red caught my eye across the way. Santa Claus was just running out the front door of A Touch of Glass, on the other side of the Bijou!

I pointed at the fleeing figure. "What the—"

"Police! Robbery!"

Lynda and I both looked toward the sound of the yelling. Loud as it was, we still probably wouldn't have heard it if there hadn't been a pause in the caroling at that moment. Clarice Stansfield, the elegant owner of A Touch of Glass, stood in the doorway of her store trying to catch the attention of the Erin constabulary. (Where had I heard her name just recently?) Within maybe half a minute or less, she succeeded. A fresh-faced young policeman, whose uniform seemed about a size too big, arrived on the scene. I'd never seen the officer before—presumably a new hire. I watched as, using a lot of hand motions, Ms. Stansfield explained the situation to him.

When she finished, the officer moved swiftly—toward us! Or at least, in our direction. As he walked, he strained his head upward like a turtle. A man of medium height, no more than about five-seven or -eight, he seemed to be looking for someone taller. Finally, he stopped in front of the Bijou and the Santa roasting chestnuts.

Lynda and I were right behind. Her journalism genes had kicked in, and I just wanted to be able to relate the whole Santa Claus Caper to Mac. As it turned out, I needn't have worried about that.

"Don't move, sir," the officer instructed the faux Santa. He lifted his service revolver, not pointing but making a point.

"I assure you, Officer, that I have neither the intention nor the ability to move. Is something amiss?"

That voice! That cadence! That vocabulary!

"Well, now you know which Santa beard Mac is hiding under," Lynda told me dryly.

"I'm placing you under arrest on suspicion of robbing A Touch of Glass," Erin's Finest responded. "You have the right to remain silent . . ." Etc. You know the rest of that drill as well as Mac did.

Not-So-Tiny Tim, sitting a couple of yards away, scrambled to his feet. "Wow, Dad, your life of crime is exposed at last!"

Please tell me this is being captured on the cop's bodycam.

Inside that Dickensian costume was our nephew, Brian, who would be fifteen if he survived to the end of February. Brian wasn't even in *A Christmas Carol.* But he has a good singing voice, so maybe he was on special loan as a caroler for the day.

Mac gave his son a murderous look, then told the officer: "I assure you that you are making a mistake. I am Professor McCabe."

"Pleased to meet you," the young cop deadpanned. "I am Officer Mentzel. May I see some ID, sir?"

He was a new hire, all right, and probably new to Erin if he didn't know Mac at least by reputation.

Mac handed over his driver's license. Mentzel took it in his gun-free left hand and gave it a glance. "Please remove the beard, sir."

Mac did so, revealing the shorter salt-and-pepper beard beneath.

"If there's any doubt, I can identify this desperado," I offered.

"Who are you, sir?"

"Thomas Jefferson Cody, of St. Benignus University."

"And I'm—" Lynda began.

"Never mind. I'm going to have to ask you both, and your children, to step back into the crowd." There was a crowd, and it was growing. "This is a police investigation."

"I'm also a witness," I added. "I saw Santa Crook running from the store. Obviously, Professor McCabe here can't run."

"Why not?"

Mac slowly stepped out from behind the grill, which had concealed the bottom half of his body. His right leg, the one with the sprained ankle, was supported on a kind of crutch while his shin was bent at a ninety-degree angle and resting on a knee pad. His pant leg was cut off, but maybe the grill kept him warm.

"That's a pretty cool contraption!" Lynda said.

"An engineering marvel," I agreed. "What's it called?"

"This is an iWalk 2.0," Mac informed us.

"Notice, it's not called an iRun," I told Mentzel. He ignored that.

"If you saw the suspect running out of the store, where did he go?"

Well, this is embarrassing. "I don't know. I stopped watching him when Clarice Stansfield—the store owner—came out and started yelling for the police."

Lynda had done the same.

Mentzel's face was unreadable. "Okay, let's see what Ms. Stansfield has to say about this."

"Call Chief Hummel," Brian suggested.

"He can vouch for Mac," Lynda said.

This advice did not seem especially welcome. Mentzel thought it over for about three seconds, then said: "The Chief's on special duty today."

"His cell number—" Mac began.

"I know his cell number." For some reason, young Mentzel sounded frustrated. Apparently deciding that Mac wasn't going anywhere, he holstered his gun and pulled out his phone. He selected "Chief" from the directory.

"Hi, Chief. Sorry to bother you. I've just arrested a robbery suspect who claims to know you. His name's McCabe." I could hear Oscar laughing from ten feet away. "Yes, sir. And he kind of has his own cheering section with him. Yeah, that's his name, Cody. Okay, I'll ask." He looked at my wife. "Your name Lynda?"

"I tried to tell you that. You want the kids' names?"

He ignored her. "Yeah, she's here. Okay, Chief." He disconnected. "The Chief says you can all stay if you promise not to cause any trouble. He'll meet us in the store. Let's go."

"One moment, please," Mac said. "I can walk in this apparatus, but I prefer not to." He unstrapped the gizmo and Brian handed him his crutches, which had served as props for Tiny Tim.

We headed toward the store, Brian included until Mac informed him, "Your services will no longer be required, young man."

"Oh, Dad! You never let me have any fun."

"I might say the same to you. However, at this particular moment we are not having a debate."

The carolers picked up again, and Brian joined them. He didn't look particularly glum, by which I realized that his protest had been purely a matter of form.

Clarice Stansfield met us at the door of A Touch of Glass, purveyor of fine crystal glassware to the gentry. In her sixties, she looks like one of those slender, sophisticated women in 1940s cigarette ads. Her hair didn't know whether it was blond or gray, but it was certainly well-coiffed.

Mentzel introduced himself and pointed at Mac. "Is this the man who robbed you, ma'am?"

"Don't be silly, Officer. That's Sebastian McCabe."

Mac bowed in her direction.

Mentzel took a deep breath. "Okay, but if he wasn't Sebastian McCabe, would he be the man who robbed you?"

She considered. "Well, he is the right size both ways, but then, all Santas are fat."

"Okay. You said the robber had a green and red pin on his hat." He pointed at Mac's, which wasn't bringing Mac any SHALOM. "That's what I was looking for when I searched the crowd."

"The Erin Interfaith Council is passing out those pins as a holiday peace greeting," I said. "Half the Santas in town are wearing them. So are we." I pointed to the one on my jacket. Lynda's was on her scarf.

"Okay, okay," Mentzel said. "Let's take this from the top, Ms.—"

"Call me Clarice."

"Okay. What exactly happened?"

"When Santa Claus came in with a 'ho-ho-ho,' I didn't think much of it. Santafest and all that. There was only one customer and me in the store at the time."

"Do you know the customer's name?"

"Mrs. Betty Tippers, but she can't tell you anything. She finished her mimosa and left before he showed the gun."

"Her mimosa," Mentzel repeated.

"I like to treat my customers well. Mimosas aren't just for breakfast, you know. Anyway, after Betty left, I was alone with Santa Claus."

"No employee?"

"David Price is working today, but he took a late lunch. Anyway, you could have knocked me over with a feather when Santa started waving a gun at me."

"What kind?"

"The kind that could kill me, I assumed. I don't know anything about guns, Officer! Anyway, he just pointed the thing at me and then at the cash register, not saying a word. I got the message. I cleaned out the drawer."

"How much was in there?"

"More than eight hundred dollars."

Mac raised an eyebrow, which he had used makeup to whiten. "That strikes me as rather a large amount of cash to have on hand, Clarice. I would have expected customers at a high-end establishment such as this to make their purchases with credit or debit cards."

Clarice nodded. "Most of them do. But one of my best customers, Everett Thompson, bought a Limited Edition Waterford Ballerina Vase for his wife this morning. That's where most of the money in the till came from. Mr. Thompson is rather elderly and always pays cash. And he always drinks *two* mimosas. I knew he was coming in today to make this particular purchase as birthday present, so I made sure I had enough orange juice and his favorite bubbly in the refrigerator."

"Ho ho ho," a voice announced glumly. We all turned around. Oscar Hummel was on the scene.

And he was dressed as Santa Claus, no padding necessary—with a green and red SHALOM pin on his pointed hat.

Chapter Twenty-Two
The Prosecutor Rests

"It was all rather amusing," I assured Popcorn. "To me, anyway."

"Oscar didn't think so," she informed me.

"Maybe if Marvin Slade gets wind of it, he won't be so eager to take us to lunch. And where did Mac get off just blithely assuming I would go along on this little field trip to some highfalutin club in Cincinnati?"

"Well, you always do go along, Boss," Popcorn said. "Besides, he needs a chauffeur these days."

A chauffeur! And I thought being a Watson was demeaning!

"Meanwhile, Santa Crook is still on the loose," I pointed out. "Mac says the solution is 'almost painfully evident,' but I think he's just posturing."

"Oscar will get him," Popcorn said loyally.

It was Monday morning of exam week, five days before the December commencement rites on Saturday. With Warren Burch waked and buried, life proceeded for the rest of us. Jason Danvers had even taken a holiday from Twitter, probably to prepare for exams. It struck me, irreverently, that the dead man's final exam for his students in "International Economics and Finance" really was his *final* exam, found among the papers on his desk. Wendy Yazane would administer it to his students this week, along with the exam for his post-graduate course on "European Monetary and Fiscal Policy."

I spent a chunk of that morning in the presidential office prepping GK for an interview he had scheduled with Maggie Barton that afternoon. He had already started to make the quarters his own with a sign on the desk proclaiming his motto: **LEADERS LEAD**. Maggie would probably ask some of the same questions as Tony Lampicke, as well as some that the university employee wouldn't dare pose. The role-playing went like this:

"How do you feel about replacing a legend?" (Softball.)

"Nobody can replace Father Joe, least of all an interim appointment like myself. But I intend to be more than a place-holder in the short time I occupy this office."

"How is the search for a new president going?" (Softball.)

"It hasn't begun yet, but it will soon. Sister Jacinta is putting together an eighteen-member committee, which will include wide representation both from the campus community and from the broader Erin community."

"How do you feel about the university's settlement with the late Warren Burch?" (Hardball.)

"At this point, Maggie, that's a moot point. The important thing is that I want to make it clear to all our faculty, staff, and students that every member of the St. Benignus family is to be treated with respect. There will be zero tolerance not just of any violation of Title IX, but of any violation of personal dignity."

And so forth.

Softball or hardball, GK hit all my practice questions out of the park. I gave him a few suggestions and a set of talking points to drag into his answers, no matter what the questions were. He had to affirm SBU's Catholic identity and its commitment to the local community, for example. If Maggie didn't bring up campus safety (unlikely), GK would do so. Best not to stress the video surveillance, since that (a) didn't help Warren Burch much, and (b) it riled up civil libertarians. But he should stress the system of Help Phones throughout the campus that provided a hotline to Campus Police for anybody in trouble.

"Got it." Grant Kingsley reached across his desk and gave me a retired-colonel handshake. "This should be fun."

Do you also enjoy swallowing razor blades?

I was back in my office an hour or so later, inserting final numbers into the news release on the December commencement, when I took a call from Banfield.

"Jeff? It's Aurelia. I had an idea that panned out and I thought you and Seb would want to know about it." She tried to sound off-hand, but it wasn't working. She was excited.

"I'm all ears."

"Okay, so, I have a friend who has a friend who's a pilot for Altiora Corp. He flies the top brass in and out of Erin Municipal Airport. And he says—the friend of a friend, that is—that he took Grant to the corporate HQ in Connecticut on Monday morning and back on Wednesday afternoon. So, Grant's alibi checks."

So that was the "c"—the third possibility other than Gibbons messing up or GK lying: Grant Kingsley didn't fly commercial. Of course, you could argue that Gibbons did mess up by not thinking of the corporate aircraft angle, but that would be picky.

"I'd call that good news, even though it doesn't help the investigation," I said. "How's Gibbons taking it?" I assumed she'd called him first.

"He'll get over it eventually."

I thanked her and hung up, feeling slightly guilty that Mac and I hadn't told her about our meetings with the fourth woman and, upcoming, with Marvin Slade. But we'd promised confidentiality in both cases. If she ever found out, she'd get over it eventually.

In deference to Mac's massive bulk, his crutches, and the forty-mile trip downriver to Cincinnati, I borrowed Lynda's yellow Mustang for the day. I tried not to look annoyed when she prayed over the thing before I left in the morning. Just for the record, I returned it without a scratch.

"At least I can move Grant Kingsley off my worry plate," I told Mac as I drove. "His alibi is solid."

"In a Golden Age detective story, an unbreakable alibi would almost guarantee his guilt," Mac observed.

"Yeah, well, good thing we're not in a detective story, Golden Age or otherwise."

But the Nonpareil Club was something out of the Gilded Age, with tall ceilings, lots of columns, and marble with gold trimmings. The painting of William Howard Taft on the first floor was about five times the size of the one in Saylor-Mackie's office. It looked like the sort of place where they would turn you away in a sniff if you weren't wearing at least a three-piece suit, if not a tux. I was disappointed that the dress code for the club's Grill Room, which I found online, permitted "business casual." For men that meant collared shirts, turtlenecks or sweaters; dress slacks, khakis or corduroy trousers; and socks. Good thing I didn't spring for a tux at the Black & White going-out-of-business sale. But I wore my best Frank Lloyd Wright tie and a blue suit anyway, and Mac showed up in tweeds and one of his customary bow ties, this one yellow with blue dots.

Marvin Slade awaited us at a table in the Grill Room. He wore a blue pinstriped suit, white shirt, and red tie. His dyed brown hair, which he'd been combing over for years, needed cutting.

"Thanks for making the trek," he said, after the usual round of handshakes.

"I assume you wished to assure the private nature of our meeting," Mac said.

"Exactly. Do I have your word that everything that was said on Friday and everything we talk about today stays strictly between us?"

"Deal," I said.

"Certainly," Mac agreed. "Assuming, of course, that you are not going to confess to a felony that we would be obligated by law to report to the proper legal authorities."

Slade glowered. Nobody ever accused him of having a sense of humor. But maybe Mac wasn't kidding.

At that point the waiter swept in with menus and all meaningful conversation ceased for several minutes as we got down to the serious business of deciding what to eat. I settled on grilled Atlantic salmon, with summer vegetable ratatouille, while Mac chose lamb chops. Prices weren't listed, but I assumed that Slade was shelling out big bucks indeed for the pleasure of our company.

He didn't wait for the salads to arrive to dive in.

"I'm sure you can imagine that this whole Warren Burch affair has been very difficult on our family," he said.

That was just the wind up, but Mac didn't wait for the pitch. "Indeed," he said, "given what your daughter suffered at Professor Burch's hands, I should think you might find it hard to prosecute his killer."

Especially if it's you, Marvin!

Slade shook his head. "I won't be doing that, not personally. I'll have one of my assistants take the case to court. I'm just too emotionally involved. And even if that weren't the case, the optics would be bad. I'm sure you understand that as prosecutor it would be well within my purview, totally appropriate, to ask how the investigation into Burch's death is going. But I would feel awkward talking to Hummel or Decker about it. I mean, I assume they know Zoe has been questioned."

"If they don't, they will," I confirmed. "Banfield reports up the chain of command."

"Sure. So, I'm asking you instead of the chiefs. How's it going?"

"The inquiry is still in the early stages," Mac said. "We know a fair amount. We may even know more than we know we know." *Right.* "However, the matter does not yet begin to assume a shape."

Slade looked exasperated right down to his gray hair roots. "You're not making this easy on me."

"I apologize."

"I was hoping to hear that the girls, Burch's victims, had been cleared so the whole issue could be avoided in the murder trial. Erica doesn't want Zoe on the stand."

"I quite understand."

"No, you don't." The quick and firm rebuttal came across like a shout, even though Slade didn't raise his voice. Just then the food came, and we took a time-out while the waiter and his help set it before us. When they left, Slade leaned forward. "She's never talked about it publicly, but Erica was abused by an older cousin when she was fourteen years old. The abuser refused to accept a plea deal and Erica had to testify. She's adamant that she doesn't want our daughter to go through that. You heard her on that subject."

"Loud and clear," I said. "And I take it that you and your ex are on the same page for a change?"

"We are. In fact, we've been spending some time together as a family recently. It's been good. So good I'm thinking about remarrying Erica. I don't know why I'm telling you two this."

I didn't know either, but I almost fell off my chair. Mac blinked, too surprised to raise an eyebrow. I wondered whether Slade had told Erica yet.

"You two didn't seem all that cozy the other day," I observed.

Slade shrugged. "It's complicated."

Tell that to Facebook.

Mac sighed. "I am sorry that we cannot yet give you the assurance that Warren Burch's depredations are unconnected to his murder. Granted, the young women involved do not seem likely suspects for various reasons." He paused. "They do have parents, however. I am sure you recall that Ms. Slade herself expressed a desire to do physical violence to Professor Burch."

Slade looked almost panicky. "But that was just talk. You know how Erica is—hard as nails on the outside." *And hard as bullets on the inside.*

He turned reflective. "I'm still stunned by all this crap. When Zoe went out for track and field as a first-year student, that worried me a little. A lot of stories were breaking in the media then, still are, about team coaches and doctors abusing college athletes—men on women, men on men, women on women, women on men. Nobody seems safe from anybody! When Zoe gave up running to concentrate on her studies, I was kind of relieved. I never dreamed that in the business school that bastard Burch—"

"Clearly, you are not a believer in *de mortuis nil nisi bonum*," Mac rumbled.

"'Of the dead say nothing but good?' No. How about, 'of the dead say nothing but truth.' Let's face it, Burch was a waste of perfectly good DNA. But I've dealt with dozens of abuse and sexual imposition cases as prosecutor, and none resulted in the perpetrator being murdered two or three years later. A few perps have been killed in the act and our office agreed that it was self-defense. None were killed by somebody other than the victim."

Slade paused to emit a sigh. "You're not helping me much, McCabe."

"Then perhaps you can help us. Who do you suggest might have killed Professor Burch?"

Slade studied his water glass, weighing his words. "You've had a lot of success dabbling in crime-solving, Mac." *Oh, now it's 'Mac'. You're making a sale.* "A lot of success. I can't deny that. But I've prosecuted hundreds of cases in my career and most of them weren't Sebastian McCabe cases. I've thought about this, and maybe you're overlooking the obvious here. The murderer didn't show up on the surveillance video—Chief Hummel told me that. Very mysterious, but there's an easy explanation. Maybe Jackson, that campus police officer who supposedly found the dead body, made the body dead instead of just finding it that way."

"Why would he do that?" I blurted out.

"It looks unpremeditated. Maybe Burch caught him doing something he shouldn't."

Chapter Twenty-Three
Murder Makes an Encore

"Well, that was informative," Mac said on the way home.

"Regarding which—the possible Slade nuptials or the prosecutor considering Jackson a suspect?"

"The latter. Nothing concerning romance ever surprises me, Jefferson, for love in all its forms is utterly irrational. As to Officer Jackson, it is true that his presence is so obvious we overlooked him, like Poe's purloined letter. He does bear further scrutiny. On the other hand, Sherlock Holmes once observed that 'there is nothing more deceptive than an obvious fact.'"

"What's in your third hand?" I quipped.

"Marvin Slade's manifest interest in diverting our attention from the objects of Professor Burch's attentions and their parents. I believe the catchphrase of the day is 'Move along, nothing to see here.'"

"Yeah, that was pretty obvious. But as the great Sherlock Holmes once said, 'there is nothing more deceptive than an obvious fact.'"

Being a careful driver, especially with the Mustang, I didn't look over to see the look on his face. But I wanted to. Payback is so much fun. I settled for a reversal of roles, telling Mac what to do for a change.

"Why don't you give Banfield a jingle and ask her about Jackson's service record?" I suggested.

He didn't grumble, I'll give him that. He whipped out his phone and called her.

"Sebastian McCabe here, Ms. Banfield. Have you a moment? Good. What can you tell us about your comrade in arms, Officer Jackson? Oh, just a notion I had." Slade would appreciate Mac keeping him out of it. "He is, after all, the one person that we know was in Mackie Hall with Professor Burch the night of the murder."

She talked, and he listened, for a good ten minutes while she spilled the beans. It was a big bag. Mac thanked her, asked her what line of inquiry she planned to pursue next, and disconnected.

"Ms. Banfield did not overlook the obvious," he reported. "Although from her personal observation she believes Henry Jackson to lack the ambition for either malfeasance or murder, she has been running the paper trail on him in spare moments. I speak metaphorically, of course. Scarcely any paper is involved. Officer Jackson is thirty-three, unmarried, tolerated but not highly regarded on the force. You recall, of course, the allegation of police brutality against him more than two years ago?"

"How could I forget?"

Lani Alvarez, president of a banned student organization called the Young Socialist Brigade, claimed that Jackson "personhandled her" during a protest against student fees going to athletics. His defense was that she got in his face in a threatening way and he shoved her back. She showed bruises on her arm all over Facebook, Pinterest, Snapchat, and Twitter. The betting in my office was that the bruises came from a boyfriend. Then it turned out that Jackson *was* the boyfriend, although she later referred to their romance as a "sociological experiment" on her part. She left SBU with a settlement and ran for mayor, finishing fourth in a three-person race. Jackson got transferred to night duty.

"He has only been patrolling that part of the campus for approximately a year, and there is no reason to believe he knew Professor Burch for any longer than that, or in any other context. He has never been accused of dishonesty.

Indeed, the fracas involving Ms. Alvarez is the only blot on his twelve-year career with the Campus Police Division. He is an adequate officer, although no more than that, which is why others have been promoted over him. Ms. Banfield believes he probably could do better if he had the ambition. Being single, perhaps he has no reason to aspire to greater authority, responsibility, and salary. He likes to gamble at the Forty Thieves Casino in Cincinnati, but not to excess. His credit rating is excellent."

"What day does he do his laundry?"

Mac ignored that.

"What emerges, Jefferson, is a portrait of a man who has adequate funds for his chosen modest lifestyle. Therefore, robbery of some unknown treasure seems unlikely. His income as a campus police officer is not great, and therefore replacing it would not be an insurmountable challenge. Thus, it is hard to see him killing to save his job, perhaps to conceal some other crime. Incidentally, along those lines, Ms. Banfield also informed me that there have been no unsolved break-ins or other crimes at the business school over the past year or in the other areas of the campus under his patrol."

"None?"

"None unsolved. Ms. Banfield is proud of her force's 'clearance rate', as she called it."

I sighed, but it was a sigh of satisfaction. "Slade can't say we didn't try."

Back at the ranch, the big work of the afternoon was sitting in on Maggie Barton's interview with Grant Kingsley. I was there to provide a fact or two if asked by either the reporter or the interim president. Also, I would take my own notes in case Maggie muffed a quote. That had been known to happen. She arrived at the anteroom outside the presidential office just a few minutes before the appointment, looking harried and old—even worse than she'd looked at the funeral home. No wonder she was thinking of hanging up her notebook. In Social Security terms, she had reached "Full Retirement Age" (FRA) during the last Bush Administration.

"Hi, Jeff. Am I late?"

"Don't worry. We can't start without you."

I swiftly ushered her into GK's presence, knowing he didn't like to waste time. She shook his hand and they exchanged the customary pleasantries of two people who had never met before. Then GK got to work, rolling up his metaphorical shirt sleeves. The military-industrial-academic leader was all energy and bonhomie. **LEADERS LEAD**, as the sign on his desk proclaimed, but they also schmooze. And I saw then that GK was very, very good at schmoozing. Within two minutes he expressed his sympathy on the death of Maggie's great-niece, assured her that he'd been reading her stories for years, and said he planned to be as available to the press as his schedule allowed.

Looking distracted and a bit nervous despite the full-court press, Maggie opened her notebook. "So, how are you settling in?"

"You know, Maggie, I can't get too settled in because I'm only interim president. At the same time, I don't intend to be a placeholder. Some big decisions can and should wait for the next president, but SBU can't just go on autopilot until one is chosen. So, there's a balance there. I intend to do what needs to be done. Fortunately, I have a great staff to help me, like Jeff here."

That's true.

"How do you feel about being named interim president?"

"I am honored and humbled by the board of trustees' confidence in me, Maggie. There are many individuals in administration here at SBU who would have done a fine job as interim, but the board didn't want to take any of them away from the important work they're doing now."

This was very good stuff. My boss's new boss was riffing wonderfully on what we'd rehearsed.

"Why did you take the position?"

"I just couldn't say no to the chance to make a difference at this critical point in the life of St. Benignus University. I'm grateful that my bosses at the Altiora Corp. let me say 'yes'."

"What do you hope to accomplish in this role?"

"My goals are to successfully launch our capital campaign, grow student enrollment by five percent, and provide a smooth transition to the next president. That should be enough to keep me challenged."

It didn't surprise me that GK would target a specific enrollment goal, but that was the first time I'd heard the number. I made a note of it.

Maggie asked a few other innocuous questions ("What's your secret talent?" "If you weren't doing this, what would you be doing?"). Then:

"How do you feel about replacing a legend?"

"Well, Maggie, nobody could ever replace Father Joe, certainly not an interim like myself."

"It must be tough taking over from a legend at a time when the university is reeling—first from my reports about Warren Burch's ouster as dean of the business school because of sexual harassment, and then his murder in his own office."

So much for the softballs. Cue the talking points on Title IX and campus security.

"Yes, this is a particularly difficult time for SBU, no question about it. And I want to make it clear to all our faculty, staff, and students that every member of the St. Benignus family is to be treated with respect. There will be zero tolerance not just of any violation of Title IX, but any violation of personal dignity. That's one of our top priorities, along with campus security. As you know, before he resigned, Father Joe rightly launched a comprehensive study—"

And so it went for the next thirty minutes or so. It was a beautiful thing to watch until it got interrupted by a familiar sound.

DA-da-da-da—DA-da-da! I pulled out my phone and looked at the screen. "It's Decker," I informed GK. That couldn't be good. Banfield would be the one calling with news on the Burch case, good or bad. With Decker it would only be bad. GK nodded, giving me permission to take the call. I made a quick exit from the room.

"What happened?" I said by way of answering the call.

"Team physician for the Lady Dragons, Dr. Helen Calloway—she was found murdered."

"In her office?" I interrupted.

"Yeah. Bashed in the head, just like Burch. The blood is still wet, and she hasn't gone into rigor yet. We've got another hot one here. The coroner is on her way."

Holy crap!

"You bring so much sunshine into my life, Ed. Okay, I'm with Grant Kingsley right now. I'll tell him."

"Good. I thought Cal should do that, but I haven't been able to reach him yet."

When I walked back into the office, GK gave me a "well?" look. There was no way to make this easy.

"There's been another murder on campus."

"What the hell!" He threw down the pen he'd been fiddling with.

"I'd better go over there—the Athletics Building. The victim is the team doc for the Lady Dragons. I just saw her on Friday at Hawes & Holder." I felt a little numb about that.

Maggie closed her notebook. "I'll go with you."

I looked at GK for a clue as to what he thought of that idea. Catching my meaning, he seemed to shrug his shoulders without moving them. "If there are any restrictions on press access to the scene of the murder, they're going to come from law enforcement, not from me. And I think Father Joe would want you to alert McCabe. Better yet, pick him up on the way."

"You might as well go on ahead while I collect Mac," I told Maggie. "You know where Athletics is?"

"I've been there."

I hustled toward Herbert Hall, calling Mac on the way.

"This is most unexpected," he noted when I'd filled him in.

"I imagine Dr. Calloway was taken aback as well," I said acidly.

"Or perhaps not, old boy. It is a capital mistake to theorize—"

I disconnected without another word, feeling pissed at him, at myself, and at the whole world. Calloway seemed like a nice sort, and just a few days ago she was at somebody else's wake.

The Athletics Building is on the other side of campus from Herbert Hall, not far from the Sports Complex. Though it's a small campus, with Mac on crutches I wished we had a golf cart. It took us twenty minutes or so to get there. We arrived to find Maggie standing outside the building, next to an EMS van, looking disgruntled.

"The cops won't let me go in," she fumed. "They say it's a crime scene."

"That does seem inarguable," Mac observed.

"And the coroner's not telling me very much."

"She probably doesn't know very much yet," I pointed out.

Maggie muttered something about public officials, freedom of the press, the right to know, yada yada yada.

Banfield logged us in at the door. "The Chief said you two are allowed. Jack's also on his way. I notified the victim's husband, Roger Calloway. Dr. Eppensteiner is expecting you."

Not that the coroner was happy to see us.

"Let's not make a habit of meeting like this," she said, pushing curly dark hair off her face. "I was hoping to have a quiet last night of Hanukkah with my husband and kids."

This didn't seem like a good time for a Cody comeback, so I kept my sarcastic mouth unopened.

Helen Calloway's office was a computer-and-paperwork hideaway, not a working doctor's office. It was warmed with plants, drapes, an art deco floor lamp, and a painting of a six-pack of basset hounds that took up most of a wall. If she examined student athletes, that must have been in some other part of the building or maybe at the Sports Complex. I made a mental note to drop in some day and get reacquainted with this part of campus when there wasn't a dead body involved.

Calloway lay on the floor, her auburn hair matted with blood that spilled over onto a beige carpet. What looked like a gallon of the red stuff was probably a cupful, not quite the same dark shade as her fingernails. She wore a pink jacket over a white blouse and a black skirt.

"This is déjà vu all over again," Eppensteiner said. "It's almost as if the murderer is signing his or her work. The subject was hit from behind, above the right ear, just like with Warren Burch. But keep that to yourself."

"Weapon?" Mac asked.

"A team trophy."

"In terms of her world, another award significant in her professional field," I said. "So that's a repeat, too."

"There is at least one difference between this murder and the last," Mac said. "We quite reasonably posited that the killing of Warren Burch lacked premeditation. It strains credulity to theorize a second spontaneous killing at the hands of the same killer."

"And it must be the same killer because of the M.O., which Dr. Eppensteiner and law enforcement haven't made public," I noted.

"Look at the bright side," Banfield said. "Now we'll be trying to find one person who would want to kill both. That should limit the field quite a bit. Plus, we'll eventually clear two cases at the same time."

That's the bright side?

"I've already dispatched two officers to try to find somebody who saw something," she continued, "but it's pretty quiet on this end of campus during exam week. That might be an advantage when we see the surveillance video— not a lot of extraneous characters, so to speak."

"Let us hope the video record will be more enlightening this time," Mac offered.

Hope is not a plan.

I needed to connect with GK and fill him in as soon as possible, if not sooner. But first, I turned to Eppensteiner. "Do yourself a favor, Arly. Throw Maggie Barton a bone. The old trouper is not going to let go of this story, so you might as well establish a good working relationship with her."

Call that my good deed for the day, although I'm not sure who it was good for.

"Oh, all right. I'll go play nice. But I'm not going to tell her much."

"I, for one, appreciate that," Banfield said. "At some point the killer might betray knowledge of information about the crime that hasn't appeared in the media. So, if you keep holding back the details, that would be a good thing for our investigation."

Dr. Eppensteiner nodded and moved toward the door. Before she got very far, though, a man with a body like a linebacker and thinning hair the color of a scarecrow's straw barreled in. Where had I seen him before? And not so long before.

"Helen!"

One of Banfield's troops tried to restrain him, to no avail. He wasn't being stopped by anybody—until he saw the body. Then he sank to his knees. "Oh, my God! It's true! Helen! Oh, my God!"

Nothing is quite so moving as the sight of a big man crying. He looked around him, bereft and bewildered all at the same time. "What the hell happened?"

"I'm sorry," Eppensteiner said. She sounded like she meant it, not like she was reading it off a cue card. "Someone struck your wife with a heavy object. She was already dead when campus police found her, responding to an anonymous call from one of the Help Phones. There was nothing anyone could do. You'd better have a seat."

He sat.

"But why? *Why?*"

"I take it you don't know anyone who would want to kill your wife?" Mac said. Banfield, caught up in the moment, forgot to look peeved that he asked a question.

Roger Calloway shook his head. "No, no, of course not."

"How well did you know Dr. Calloway?" Banfield asked. "I mean, were you married a long time?"

"Five years. We were both in second marriages."

"Any tension with previous spouses?"

"No, not at all. Helen's first husband divorced her. They got along much better after that. I was a widower."

"No custody conflicts over children?" Eight members of one family in rural Ohio were massacred in 2016 over a custody issue.

"No, our children were grown when we married."

Only later did it occur to me that grown children might be the source of other kinds of conflict in a blended family.

Banfield asked the name of the first husband anyway, and Calloway served it up—Bradford Connors.

That line of questioning played out for the time being, Banfield moved on to the double-murder angle:

"You may be aware of another murder on campus last week," she said. *Isn't everybody?* "Did you have any connection, anything at all, with Warren Burch?"

"Yes, certainly. He was an investor in my business, Canine College. But what could that possibly have to do with Helen's murder?"

"Maybe nothing. In a town this size, everybody has about two degrees of separation instead of six. But it's a place to start."

Something in the way he turned his head from her to look at his lost wife reminded me of where I'd seen Roger Calloway before: It was at Hawes & Holder, outside of Burch's wake on Friday night. He was the man to whom Evan Farleigh gave a pill.

Chapter Twenty-Four
Connections

"I knew there was something I forgot to tell you about the funeral home," I informed Mac on our way to his house. Our departure from the Athletics Building had followed Roger Calloway formally identifying the body, Gibbons arriving on the scene, and Maggie managing to extract quotes from everybody of consequence by patiently waiting for them outside.

Mac cocked an eyebrow. "And you find this significant? What do you suspect?"

"Suspect? You've got to be kidding me! It's as plain as the beard on your face!"

"Obvious, in fact?"

"Right. It's all about drugs, probably prescription opioids. We know there was a business connection between Burch and Roger Calloway. Maybe there was also a drug connection, as in Burch was his supplier—until Farleigh, who must have known about it all along, killed Burch and took over his sideline in pharmaceuticals. As his attorney and illegal business partner, he might have visited him in his office and been familiar with it. Certainly, he was on campus while negotiating the Burch settlement. So that gives us the SBU angle we were looking for. Do you see any holes in that?"

"One or two, old boy. Where does the murder of Helen Calloway fit it?"

"She's our old friend The Woman Who Knew Too Much. Assume my theory is correct. If Roger Calloway knew or had strong reason to believe that Farleigh killed Burch, he wouldn't tell anybody because that would cause his supply to get cut off. You know how far addicts will go to feed their habit. I just read a couple of weeks ago about an Ohio cop who turned into a robber to get drugs when his insurance company stopped covering the cost of pain pills. The poor devil hurt his back on the job when he was fighting with a guy who tried to take his service weapon away. Ironic and sad, isn't it?"

"Tragically so. And Dr. Calloway?"

"Oh, right. She could have known, or strongly suspected, that Farleigh killed Burch and—unlike her husband—had no compunction about turning him in. She might have even seen that as a way to force her husband into treatment for his addiction."

I was on fire!

"Ingenious, Jefferson! However, you have built a rather large house for such a small foundation. You observed just one pill change hands, remember."

"Maybe I'm wrong here, but I don't think drug dealers trade in big boxes of the stuff like Sam's Club."

Mac appeared unmoved. But, then, that's how mountains are. "Then there is the question of why Roger Calloway would turn to a hypothesized drug dealer when he was married to a physician—in fact, one who offered to write me a prescription for a powerful painkiller upon slight acquaintance!"

"That's just it, Mac—slight acquaintance. With her husband, and knowing that he'd become addicted, it would be different."

"By thunder, you have an answer for everything!"

"Yes, I do." I could feel myself smile. And the best thing about my theory was that the damage to St. Benignus University would be minimal.

"The damage to St. Benignus University from this second murder is incalculable," Grant Kingsley declared, sitting at his desk below a newly mounted painting of Air Force jets flying in formation. The starch seemed to have left his shirt. "No parents want to send their kids to a college where people keep getting whacked."

Tuesday morning, the day after Helen Calloway's murder, the interim president and I were doing a full sit-down status assessment. This came on the heels of hours of phone and text interaction. In between which, I lightly edited Lynda's splendid profile for *Ben* magazine: "Fr. Joseph Pirelli: Father of his University." I'm in the communications business.

"It doesn't look great," I admitted, "but when I think back at the murders Mac and I have been involved in over the past seven years, and where they took place, SBU is as safe as any place in Erin."

"That's cold comfort, Jeff! Besides, perception is everything."

Clichés generally get to be clichés because they're true, and I couldn't debunk that one. And a highly negative perception of the university was being stoked by media, both social and legacy. Jason Danvers, who should have been studying for exams, had returned to the twitterverse to tweet: "*More murder on the SBU campus. When will it stop? Who of us is safe?*" Hadley Reams of the *Spectator* was a little more restrained with a quick online editorial: "We take Interim President Grant Kingsley at his word that campus security is his top priority. However, good intentions are not enough." And so forth. Hadley was probably miffed that GK hadn't yet sat for an interview with him, as he had for Maggie and Lampwicke.

The innocuous *Crosscurrents* interview would be broadcast on our campus station that day, which if not greatly helpful at least wouldn't hurt anything.

And then there was the *Observer*, with the six-column headline **SBU SPORTS DOC MURDERED**. Maggie had the byline to herself on this one, which began:

For the second time in less than a week, an employee of St. Benignus University has been murdered on campus.

Dr. Helen Calloway, 48, team physician for the NAIA champion Lady Dragons basketball team, the track and field team, and several other women's sports teams, was found bludgeoned to death in her office on Monday.

"The SBU community is once again devastated by a tragedy," said T. Jefferson Cody, university communications director. "Our prayers are with Dr. Calloway's husband, the rest of her family, her colleagues, and the student athletes she served."

Rev. Juan Diego Garcia, director of campus ministries, will preside at a memorial Mass for the campus community on Friday.

Calloway was struck from behind on the right side of her head. Aurelia Banfield, assistant chief of SBU Campus Security, declined to comment on parallels to the murder last Wednesday night of Warren Burch, the controversial former dean of the Gulliver Mackie School of Business and Economics, who was also bludgeoned to death.

"That remains to be seen," she said. "The investigation of Professor Burch's death is ongoing in cooperation with the Erin Police Department, and we will pursue the Calloway murder on the same basis."

Burch was forced to step down as dean in 2017 when . . .

I cannot tell a lie: Banfield had a little help from yours truly by way of talking points before Maggie interviewed her.

"How about if you make a statement to the campus community," I suggested to GK, "something we can blast out on Facebook, email, Twitter, the website, the whole nine yards? Something to let them know you understand their concerns and you're on top of this."

His head was nodding before I finished. "Okay, good."

"But it can't be just pretty words, or that will be evident. What can we do beyond what we're doing already — increasing patrols and setting up the task force to review safety procedures? Not just for show, but to really make a difference?"

That was a high bar I was setting. If there was anything that could improve security in any meaningful degree, wouldn't we have already done it?

GK drummed his fingers on the desk. "Got it! We can post a guard in every building. Altiora started doing that in all of our installations after some lunatic shot up a bank in downtown Hartford near corporate headquarters."

"Won't that cost a lot?"

"Not as much as not doing it. I'll get Cal Daley to work on costing that out, while you work on wrapping some words around the announcement. But what will calm people down more than anything is solving these murders. You've already told me what you and Mac know. Now, what are you thinking?"

"Since you asked . . ."

I told him about Farleigh giving Roger Calloway a pill at Hawes & Holder, and the theory I spun off that.

"And what does McCabe think about your scenario?"

"He's not yet convinced."

GK looked surprised. "Really? I would have thought he'd be all over that fairy tale, being a fiction writer." *Ouch.* "So, what's next in the investigation?"

"Mac and I are meeting with Banfield and Gibbons later this morning at her office."

***

"The surveillance video shows a person of indeterminate sex, dressed in a loose-fitting black hoodie, entering and leaving the Athletics Building at the relevant time," Banfield shared. "There wasn't a lot of other action going on at that time of day, so it's almost certainly our killer. But we can't see a face. Even the body shape is unclear. All I can tell you is that the suspect isn't very tall."

"Does it not strike you as a significant factor that the suspect appears at all?" Mac said. "That is a departure from the pattern set in Warren Burch's murder."

"Not really," Gibbons said. "I'm starting to think that whatever happened with the Mackie Hall video was just an aberration, some kind of fluke."

"Or maybe it's not," I speculated. "Maybe the killer not appearing on the video last time was a kind of magic trick. Haven't you told me more than once, Mac, that a magician shouldn't repeat a trick to the same audience?"

He nodded. "I am impressed that you actually listened. Still, this is a point of difference in two murders that are otherwise quite similar."

"Similar enough to cause heebie-jeebies on campus," Banfield noted. "We're getting a big uptick in service calls from jumpy students, faculty, and staff who think somebody else is acting suspiciously."

"That's what's called closing the barn door, Aurelia," Gibbons said. "On the part of the callers, I mean. No criticism of your team. Let's think this through. Do we know anything about the killer other than the fact that he or she has a consistent M.O.?"

"The killer, although familiar with campus, is most likely not someone who walks these pathways every day," Mac said.

I was damned if I was going to ask how he figured that, but Banfield had it right away:

"A regular member of the campus community, like a student or a teacher, wouldn't be afraid of being seen and therefore wouldn't need a disguise," Banfield said. "He or she is part of the wallpaper."

"Precisely."

Right after Burch's murder, Mac had made a similar argument about Saylor-Mackie—that she would be so familiar as to be invisible, like the "Invisible Man" letter carrier in one of Chesterton's Father Brown stories.

"We can also assume that the killer is somehow connected to both Burch and Calloway," Banfield said.

I knew two people who fit that bill. "Both victims knew Roger Calloway, one by business and one by matrimony, and both knew Evan Farleigh." I reported what I saw at the funeral home, skipping the theorizing. If they couldn't connect the dots . . .

"If Dr. Calloway was at Burch's wake, that's a connection directly to him," Gibbons said.

"But not a big one," I countered, "and maybe not so direct. I mean, the fact that she was there doesn't necessarily have any great significance. Fred Gaffe goes to every funeral in Erin. Dr. Calloway could have been there just because her husband was."

Without comment on that, Banfield took a different tack on Helen Calloway. "Maybe she saw something on the night of Burch's murder that made her dangerous to the killer," Banfield said. "The Athletics Building is probably less than a hundred yards away from Mackie Hall. I'll check her work schedule."

"Doubtful that she'd be working that late." I didn't enjoy being so negative, but I called 'em as I saw 'em.

"We can ask her husband," Mac said. "Surely an interview with him is in order."

"Okay," said Gibbons, "let's try this from the angle of motive. The business motive for Burch's murder didn't pan out. Payback for his harassment of young women doesn't look that promising, although I don't think it's completely off the table. What if Dr. Calloway, in her role as team coach, was also putting her eyes and hands where they shouldn't be?"

I don't think Aurelia liked the jaunty way you put that, Jack.

"Don't waste your time with that one," I said. "When Maggie Barton landed on me about the Burch statement, I made sure to catch up on any Title IX violations in our files. And I paid special attention to athletics because abuse of student athletes was in the news a lot earlier this year. Therefore, I can tell you we've had no reports of inappropriate behavior by Dr. Calloway, not even perceived boundary issues."

"But we know all victims sometimes don't report, or not for years," Banfield said.

"Fair point," I conceded.

But nobody thought we should start there. We brainstormed other possible connections between the two victims—business (certainly), romance (conceivably), clubs, church, politics, hobbies, faculty committees.

We decided that Gibbons, with Mac and me in tow, would interview Roger Calloway and then circle back on Mrs. Burch.

"Whatever links their spouses might share, those two undeniably have at least one thing in common," Mac said. "They are both now free to re-marry."

Chapter Twenty-Five
Suspicions

Canine College, a single-story white frame building on the edge of town, didn't look like a thriving concern to me. It was about as quiet as a small university campus during exam week.

A tall black man and a German shepherd were just coming out of the building as we approached the walkway leading to it. The dog panted merrily, about as threatening as a beagle. Out of context and out of uniform, I didn't recognize the owner right away. But Mac did.

"Officer Jackson!"

"Oh, hello, Professor, Jeff."

"Small world," I observed.

"No, just a small town," Mac said. "Is that noble fellow a K-9?"

Jackson laughed—ruefully, I thought. "Not even close! That's the problem. I had a break-in at home last week and Bruno didn't even bark."

"Ah, the dog did nothing in the night-time! Undoubtedly, he knew the intruder. A former spouse or paramour perhaps?"

"What? No, no, no. Nothing like that. The burglar was a habitual offender named Pete Wilcox." Mac raised two eyebrows at having one of his most treasured examples of Sherlockismus blown to bits by this mundane solution. "From what I hear," Jackson went on, "this Wilcox has spent more time in the Erin jail than Chief Hummel's cleaning crew."

"Only a slight exaggeration." Gibbons almost smiled. "Pete's been booked so often I'm a little vague on his latest arrest."

"It went down like this: I'm minding my own business, drinking a beer and watching *It's a Wonderful Life* up in my bedroom on my off day, when I hear him trying to break in downstairs. So, I grab my service revolver and foil his nefarious plan." This last was said in a jokey tone. "But Bruno doesn't even whimper through the whole deal, see. How does that look for a sworn officer's animal to sleep through a burglary at his own home? I can't afford to get him trained as an attack dog, but I'm hoping this place can at least train him to bark at a home invasion."

"One would hope," Mac agreed.

"Hey, anything new on the Burch murder?"

"On that point, Officer Jackson, we remain coy at this particular juncture."

Translation: Not really.

Gibbons remained silent.

Bruno licked my hand, prompting Jackson to yell something at the dog in German and drag him away. The rest of us went into the building.

The formerly brawny Roger Calloway, the owner of Canine College, looked deflated, his thinning hair sticking out like real straw. He looked ten years older than when I'd first seen him at Hawes & Holder. We met in an untidy office by appointment. Judging by the apparent dearth of clientele, he probably had a lot of open spaces in his calendar.

"Look, you people," Calloway began by way of opening salvo, "I don't know who would want to kill Helen, and I sure as hell don't know who would want to kill both Warren *and* Helen. They barely knew each other."

"She was at his funeral visitation," Gibbons said.

He shook his head. "No, she wasn't."

"We saw her there," I blurted out.

"She was at *Mallory Lambert's* wake, the girl in the next room that night. A former Lady Dragon. Helen was her team doctor."

"Then the only connection between the two victims would seem to be you," Mac said. "You had a business relationship with Professor Burch."

Calloway looked at Gibbons. "We went through this when you came to see me last week. I put in my thirty years at Malcolm C. Cotton High and retired to do this because I've always loved dogs and Erin didn't have an obedience school. But I didn't quite have enough money. Warren filled the gap. End of story."

"How did you know him before that?" Mac asked.

"We have the same attorney, Evan Farleigh."

Ah-ha! This was the perfect time for me to say:

"I saw you and Farleigh together at the funeral home. He gave you a pill."

"So? What's that got to do with anything."

"It's been suggested"—*by me!*—"that the pill in question was a controlled substance."

This was new territory for Gibbons. His impassive face almost showed interest.

"You mean, like, drugs?" Calloway said. "Man, you people are really chasing down the wrong rabbit hole. I hate drugs. Did you know that some sick bastards hurt their dogs so that they can get prescriptions from the vet and then use the drugs themselves? It's like a thing. I read about it in the paper. It makes me sick. What Evan gave me was just a Tum-Eze for acid indigestion. It was an act of mercy. I hurt so bad I thought I was having a heart attack or something. Evan asked me what was wrong. I told him and he gave me the tablet, said he takes them all the time."

This sounded so credible it threw me for a loop. I didn't even think to ask whether the Tum-Eze worked. But Mac moved on without skipping a beat:

"What happens to your business agreement now that Professor Burch is deceased?"

Calloway looked startled. "I guess I owe the money to his widow. I hope she doesn't want it back."

"Do you know her?"

"No, not really. I've met her once or twice. Why are you asking all these questions about Burch?" He looked at Gibbons again. "Didn't I already make it clear to you that I don't profit in any way by his death? Maybe just the opposite if Catherine calls the loan. Besides, I was home with Helen the night he was killed."

"She can't verify that now," I pointed out. I must admit that was not my finest hour.

Calloway regarded me homicidally.

"Dr. Calloway backed up her husband before she died," Gibbons reported. "By the way, Mr. Calloway, where were you when your wife was killed?"

"The same place I was when the campus police called me that day—here." His tone of voice didn't just have an edge; it had a whole blade. "Do you need names of clients who saw me?"

Rex, Duke, Ranger, Bandit . . .

"That won't be necessary. Not right now."

"I resent this insulting waste of time. What are you doing to find Helen's killer?"

"Everything we can."

"That's not enough."

"Okay," I said later, "I admit my whole drug theory doesn't look good if Calloway's telling the truth."

"What drug theory?" Gibbons asked.

I laid it out for him.

"Oh."

"But I still wonder whether Calloway knows Catherine Burch better than he wants us to believe. Mac might be on to something there. Those two are both in their fifties—closer in age to each other than to their spouses. Or how about this: What if there was something going on between Burch and Helen Calloway, and her husband ended it with extreme prejudice?"

"I forgot to mention it to you," Gibbons said, "but I asked Fred Gaffe about a possible triangle involving those couples. He hasn't heard a whisper."

"Then of whispers there are none," Mac said. I know what he was thinking: No gossip worth repeating gets past the Old Gaffer, even if it doesn't all get into his *Observer* column. Considering the murder rate in this town, and the things that he knows, I wouldn't want to be Fred's life insurance agent.

"Still," I said, "those old-money types like the Harridans, Catherine Burch's family, can be amazingly discrete about things like that."

"Oh, here's a text from Aurelia," Gibbons said. He read through it quickly. We were still in his cruiser. "Helen Calloway left her office in the early afternoon the day of Burch's murder, which was typical of her working hours. That's according to her admin. There's no indication she came back later." After hours—5 P.M. or later—she would have let herself in with an electronic key. That would have been recorded. "Also, Aurelia checked the Outlook calendars and the smartphone calendars of both victims." *Of course she did.* "Neither one shows appointments with the other."

"In other words," I said, "dead ends."

"I'd prefer to put it that we've investigated and discounted those particular lines of inquiry, which means that we're that much further along in the investigation."

"Whatever." *Dead ends.*

"Now what?" Catherine Harridan Burch snapped.

Maybe we interrupted her nap. She didn't look it, though. Her ash-blond hair was well-coiffed, and her makeup was intact. She would have been pretty, in a mature way, if her mouth hadn't been pointed in the wrong direction. I'm pretty sure that soft gray dress with subtle red stripes going both horizontally and vertically never saw the inside of a Wal-Mart, either on sale or on her. It didn't offer a cold shoulder, but she did.

"We tried to call ahead," Gibbons told her apologetically.

"What could you possibly ask me about that you haven't asked me about already, Officer?"

That's Lieutenant Colonel or Assistant Chief!

Maybe it was her attitude that made me jump in with, "The other murder."

Her professionally penciled eyebrows showed surprise. "I know nothing about—Oh, come on in and let's get this over with. Wipe your feet."

Mrs. Burch took us to the sunken living room, where we three settled into the too-low couch and she perched herself on a mid-century modern chair. The chair was plush linen, dark gray like her dress, and she almost disappeared into it. She crossed her legs, waiting. She looked like she should be smoking a cigarette, but I saw no ashtrays in the house.

"I'm sure it hasn't escaped your notice that Dr. Calloway was murdered in a way very similar to your husband," Gibbons began.

"That's what I read."

"Naturally, this has us wondering about the connections between the two victims."

"So far as I know, there was none. Warren never mentioned that woman."

"But he did invest in her husband's business."

"Yes, that's true. Canine College was one of the company names I gave you. Do you really think that venture had anything to do with the murders?"

"We can't discount the possibility. But we're also looking for other angles to explore." *Meaning we're fishing in a dry hole with no bait.* "Can you think of any other links between the two at all—church, clubs, anything like that?"

"No, I—" She stopped, thought about it, and shook her head. "No. I can't think of any. Certainly, we didn't socialize with the Calloways. They were not in our set, you understand. The only connections I can think of between Helen Calloway and Warren are her husband and the university."

Incoming! My smartphone was set to vibrate, and it vibrated. A text from Popcorn let me know that she had fielded several media calls about our news release announcing the new security measures. It wasn't anything she couldn't handle, so she handled it, but wanted to let me know about it. I sent her back a thumbs up.

"Then you were not acquainted with Roger Calloway?" Mac asked.

"If I ever met the man in my life, I've forgotten it. Is he a suspect or a—what do you call it?—person of interest in the murders?" She aimed her question at Gibbons.

When Oscar Hummel plays poker on Wednesday nights, his assistant chief is not at the table for good reason. His face gave no clue.

"I'd prefer not to use such words at this point in our investigation," he said.

"What investigation? If the questions you've asked me are any indication of the way you're proceeding, no wonder you're not getting anywhere. And the campus police are no better—they took Warren's phone. What good is that? I demand that you solve the murder of my husband!"

Don't say, "We're doing the best we can."

"I understand your frustration, Mrs. Burch," Gibbons said. "Law enforcement would like to clear every case on the first day. But building a case is a little like building a house: For a long time, it looks from the outside like nothing's happening, and then it comes together at the end very quickly. I'm confident that the Erin and SBU forces, working together, will establish who killed your husband and Dr. Calloway to the satisfaction of a jury. Our goal isn't just to identify the killer but to convict him. Building the case to do that may take a little while."

"Let's hope nobody else dies in the meantime."

We're on the same page there, Mrs. B!

"Thanks for your co-operation," Gibbons said, as if she'd been co-operating.

"That's it?"

"For now. Unless you have anything else you want to tell us."

She gripped the sides of her chair. "This has been very hard for me, Officer. I hope you can understand that and excuse my impatience. If I think of anything helpful, I'll give you a call. I still have your card from the first visit."

We didn't linger long after that. And we had barely cleared the threshold of the Burch house when Gibbons held out his phone for Mac and me to see a photograph of a hoodie.

"Aurelia found it in a trash bin," he said, sounding proud. "It's what the killer's wearing in the surveillance video."

Chapter Twenty-Six
Stirring It Up

If you think that was a big break in the case, think again.

"The hoodie and the sweatpants we found with it were well worn, no tags," Banfield reported at our next confab. "I'm guessing the killer bought them at one of our finer thrift shops."

That's where I buy most of my clothes.

"I sent it all off to BCI[8] for analysis, but don't hold your breath."

The next morning, Wednesday, Evan Farleigh showed up at EPD headquarters to see Oscar and Gibbons. Mac and I weren't there, but Gibbons tells me it went something like this:

FARLEIGH: "Why are you harassing my client, Roger Calloway?"

OSCAR: "We're not harassing anybody. We're conducting a murder investigation."

FARLEIGH: "You talked to my client at the scene of his wife's murder. Why was it necessary to hound him again later in his place of business?"

GIBBONS: "There was no hounding. We had more questions as the investigation developed. Here's a question for you: Where were you during the two murders?"

FARLEIGH: "Is that a joke?"

---

[8] The Ohio Bureau of Criminal Identification and Investigation operates three crime labs and assists local law enforcement throughout the state.

OSCAR: "Gibbons doesn't joke."

FARLEIGH: "At the time of Warren's murder on Tuesday, December 4, I was at home watching television. On Wednesday, December 10, in the late afternoon, I was in my office downtown. Satisfied?"

GIBBONS: "What were your relations with Professor Burch?"

FARLEIGH: "I represented him in matters pertaining to his removal as dean of the SBU business school."

GIBBONS: "What were your relations with Dr. Calloway?"

FARLEIGH: "There were none. I only met her once or twice in my capacity as her family attorney and her husband's attorney in business affairs."

GIBBONS: "Do you happen to have a Tum-Eze on you?"

FARLEIGH: "What the hell?"

GIBBSONS: "It's an antacid tablet."

FARLEIGH: "I know what it is, damn it! I live on the stuff. But why are you asking me that?"

OSCAR: "Maybe you just give my assistant chief indigestion, counselor."

FARLEIGH: "Here. Take the damned pill, Gibbons. I seem to be on a roll giving these away."

"Calloway could have warned Farleigh that question might be coming so he'd have the Tum-Eze handy," I told Gibbons as he related the interchange. He just looked at me. This was during a conference with Mac and Banfield that afternoon.

"We seem to have made scant progress," Mac said.

"Time will tell," Banfield platitudinized. "You guys got it on the record from Catherine Burch and Roger Calloway that they barely know each other. Likewise, Evan Farleigh and Mrs. Burch. If any of those people turn out to be lying about that, it would be significant."

"If," Gibbons said gloomily.

"What about the search for the owner of the hoodie?" I asked. "Have you had any response?"

The key portion of the surveillance video had been posted on the SBU and Erin police websites, with links posted on all known social media. It had also been shown on TV4 Action News in Cincinnati—five seconds of tape which was hyped a total of twenty seconds (I added it up) during the half-hour leading up to its broadcast. There was even a still shot in that morning's *Observer*. In all media, anyone with information was asked to contact Gibbons.

"The usual thing," he said. "Seven eager citizens have turned in a neighbor so far. Four students are sure they saw the killer that afternoon and reliably reported that the figure in the hoodie was a male, a female, an Asian, an African-American, and a Caucasian."

No Native American?

So, there we were, stuck in a ditch two days post-Calloway and eight days post-Burch. But Mac thought he saw a way to get us out.

"A great detective once said the following: 'When everything seems like a hopeless mess, the thing to do is to stir it up good. Then something always comes to the top that you can use.'"

"Sherlock Holmes?" Banfield guessed.

"Close, but no pipe," I quipped. I knew what was coming because Mac briefed me in advance. I didn't dare tell them the name of the book he quoted.[9]

"Those are the words of one of the Master's great disciples, Freddy the pig."

"The pig," Gibbons repeated tonelessly. "As in bacon on the hoof?"

"Yes, but no ordinary pig! Freddy is also a detective, a magician, an author—"

---

[9] *Freddy and the Men from Mars* (Overlook Press, 2002, but first published in 1954).

"In short," said Banfield, "your role model." *They're even built along the same lines.* "I suppose you brought up this quote because you have an idea for 'stirring it up'?"

"I do. What is it that everyone on campus from first-year students to Grant Kingsley most fears, Aurelia?"

"Another murder, of course."

"Precisely! And yet, if we could provoke another murder, we might be able to catch the killer."

"Now, why didn't I think of that?" Gibbons deadpanned. "Why settle for just two murders when we could have three?"

"There will be no third murder, of course. I am talking about setting a trap."

"What's the cheese?" Banfield asked.

"I am. My idea is to give our friends in the Fourth Estate, primarily the *Observer & News-Ledger* and the *Spectator,* the impression that I know the identity of the double-murderer, but I am not yet ready to reveal it to anyone. Given my *curriculum vitae* of crime-solving, I believe it is not immodest of me to say that would loom as a credible threat to the killer. And he, or she, who has killed twice surely would not hesitate to kill a third time to protect that secret."

"We can't protect you 24/7 for very long," Gibbons warned.

"I do not think this will take very long. And I believe it is most likely to take place on campus. Either of the other two murders could have taken place elsewhere, but they did not."

"Kate will love this idea," I said, employing the well-oiled Cody sarcasm.

"This is a plan born of desperation, Jefferson. I see no need to disturb Kate's equanimity with the details."

There was some hemming and hawing, but the words "you can't do this" were not uttered. So, Mac had me take to the phones. I called Maggie Barton and Hadley Reams, starting with Maggie. I held the phone so that Mac could hear both ends of the conversation. That wasn't hard with Maggie. Being a little hard of hearing, she speaks loudly:

"Hi, Maggie. It's Jeff."

"Howdy. Are you calling about commencement or crime?"

"The latter. I wanted to tell you that Mac knows who the killer is." *But I'm not actually telling you that, because that would be a lie. Mac and I make a game of trying to avoid lying.*

There was a loud silence, then: "He does?"

"Don't sound so surprised. It wouldn't be the first time."

"Of course not. Why are you calling me?" The old gal sounded almost wary. Would I ever steer her wrong?

"Just being nice. I thought you might appreciate the tip."

"Oh! Sure. Thanks! So, he didn't give you the name?"

"He won't even tell the cops. You know him—he's probably saving it for a dramatic last scene."

Mac scowled at me. Good thing she couldn't hear that.

"But you think he'll say something for publication?"

"It's worth the old college try."

She thanked me, and we disconnected. Before I even had a chance to move on to calling Hadley, Mac's phone belted out "The Ride of the Valkyries" and it was Maggie. He put her on speaker phone.

After brief preliminaries, she moved quickly on to: "I understand you think you know who's responsible for the campus murders."

"I may." *Or I may not.*

"Anybody I know?"

"Ah, that would be telling. Prudence dictates that I not reveal the name of the killer of Professor Burch and Dr. Calloway just yet. However, after one final link in the chain is supplied, I will be ready to make that identification."

"What do you think I should do about that?"

"You may print what I just said, if you feel so inclined. It would not unduly disturb me to give the killer a sleepless night."

Both the *Observer* and *Spectator* played up Mac's supposed knowledge in a follow-up story on the search to find the person in the hoodie.

The Erin Observer & News-Ledger and the *Online Observer*, **POLICE STUMPED, NOT PROF**, by Maggie Barton and Johanna Rawls:

> Efforts by the Erin Police Department and St. Benignus University Police Division to identify the person shown in surveillance photos entering the SBU Athletics Building around the time of Dr. Helen Calloway's murder there have so far proved fruitless.
>
> "Sometimes it takes a while for the right person to come forward with key information," said L. Jack Gibbons, Erin's assistant police chief. "Assistant Chief Banfield of the campus police and I appreciate all the responses we've already had from people trying to be helpful."
>
> But Sebastian McCabe, a member of the SBU faculty best known as Erin's mystery writer and successful amateur sleuth, thinks he knows who killed Dr. Calloway and, earlier, SBU professor and former dean Warren Burch.
>
> "Prudence dictates that I not reveal the name of the killer just yet," he said. "However, after one final link in the chain is supplied, I will be ready to make that identification."
>
> Warren Burch, who was forced to resign as dean in 2017 because of . . .

That one final link, of course, was the killer trying to bag Sebastian McCabe.

The Spectator, **KILLER CAPTURE NEAR,** by Hadley
Reams:

> Although campus surveillance video has
> failed to identify the killer of Dr. Warren Burch,
> professor of business and economics, and Dr.
> Helen Calloway, team physician for the Lady
> Dragons and other women's sports, Professor
> Sebastian McCabe thinks he knows who it is.
> But he's not telling—yet.
> "I will not announce the name of the
> killer now for reasons that will become clear
> later," he told the *Spectator.*
> When asked whether he shared his
> information with law enforcement authorities,
> McCabe said, "They do not know the identity of
> the killer, so far as I am aware."
> Aurelia Banfield, assistant chief of the St.
> Benignus University Police Division . . .

The stories hit online early Thursday morning.

And then nothing happened.

By that I mean that no one tried to bonk Mac on the
head, either at his office or at home. The officers in casual
clothes who had him under surreptitious surveillance must
have been as disappointed as he was.

No doubt the routine police work of the two police
forces continued, not to mention the Banfield-Gibbons
liaisoning after hours, but we had no further conferences
over the next few days. It would be nice to report that BCI
came through with DNA from skin cells found in the collar
of the hoodie, but that didn't happen until after the killer
confessed.

Even though no one was arrested in the murders,
exam week limped to its quiet conclusion with nary a nasty
tweet from Jason Danvers and like-minded malcontents.

Mac graduated on Friday from crutches to a handsome wooden walking stick with a top carved in the shape of a hound dog's head.

"Is that a sword cane or a gun cane?" I asked.

"Neither, old boy. It does, however, provide some new options for personal defense. Now that I am somewhat more mobile, I should like to visit A Touch of Glass."

"Returning to the scene of your crime, eh?"

The store clerk was thirty-something, about Mac's height of five-ten, with a harried expression on his face as he processed a credit card payment for an older woman with impossibly black hair. The Cody memory banks accessed his name as David Price, the employee who was on break at the time of the Santafest robbery.

"It is as I expected," Mac told me after one look at him. Then he said to Price, "Ms. Stansfield?"

"She's in the back. Be out in a few minutes, I'm sure."

When she came out and saw Mac, her face lit up. "You have news about the robber?"

"It will be news to you, although I have known since the day of the robbery. Perhaps we should discuss this in your office."

"Okay. Hold down the fort, David."

"Right."

In the back office, Mac didn't waste any time hitting her with it. "The robber targeted this store at the very day there was a large amount of cash on hand and at the very time your one employee was absent. I immediately realized that he was either extraordinarily lucky, or he had inside information. The latter seemed more likely. There was only one person other than yourself who had that information."

"David?" She sounded hurt. "You're saying he was the Santa Claus robber? But he wouldn't know one end of a gun from the other!"

"It may well have been a toy. Mr. Price is the right height, a key description that Officer Mentzel focused on when he arrested me. I came here today to verify that. And why did the felonious Santa Claus not speak? Because he feared you might have recognized his voice, even if he tried to disguise it."

"You've told the police this?"

"I thought I would leave it to you to tell the authorities—or not tell them, if you so choose. It is, after all, the season of forgiveness."

She went to the door of her office and peeked out at Price showing somebody a set of crystal glasses.

"I don't know about forgiveness. I'm pretty pissed off right now. He's been like a son to me."

"I have forgiven my son many times, as my father did me."

"David's wife is very sick," Clarice Stansfield said softly, as if to herself. "Health insurance doesn't cover everything. If only he'd asked . . ."

"He made an incredibly bad decision. Judging by the anxiety I noted in his demeanor when he saw me, I suspect that he knows that. Well, the next step is yours, Clarice."

That was Friday. We never heard any more about the matter, which was good news for David Price—not his real name, by the way.

December commencement took place on Saturday. Shortly after the last diploma was handed out, I got a call from Johanna Rawls.

"Somebody who should have stopped drinking after the second beer at The Speakeasy last night told me that the so-called 'inconclusive' surveillance video didn't show a suspect going into Mackie Hall on the night Burch died. He said the only people who went in were Burch, the cleaning crew, and the night security guy. Can you confirm that?"

"No, I can't confirm that."

"Then you deny it?"

"I didn't say that."

"You mean you can neither confirm nor deny it?"

"Don't quote me on that."

"Well, thanks a heap!"

"Always glad to help the media."

Sunday afternoon, a few hours after Mass, found Sebastian McCabe and me in his study. With books on all four walls, a wet bar with a beer tap, a flat-screen television, a working desk, and a fireplace, I insist it's a man cave even though the very unmanly Kate and Lynda were ensconced in front of the fire as well.

"I simply cannot understand why no one has tried to kill me," Mac said.

"That's puzzled me for years," I assured him.

Lynda rolled her eyes.

"Only you would be upset about that," Kate told her husband. "I'm actually quite pleased nobody dispatched you, sweetheart. I'd hate to break in a new cook."

"The killer's lack of action must itself be a clue," Mac rolled on. "What can it mean?"

"It seems to me like you've got clues out the ying-yang—too many clues," I said. "The problem is figuring out what they mean."

"Precisely, Jefferson! You have put your finger on it precisely." He drank deeply of his Edmund Fitzgerald Porter. "The dog did nothing in the night-time in the famous Sherlock Holmes story because the canine knew the thief and therefore did not bark." *Do you really want to bring up that story?* "Why did the killer in this case do nothing to me in the night-time, the daytime, or anytime? It can only be that my claim of being a threat to the killer was not believable. How did the killer know that I do not know his or her identity?"

Who knows?

Lynda pointed to a stack of newspapers on the table in front of the love seat, topped by the one displaying that day's long Sunday feature on Grant Kingsley by Maggie Barton. "Maybe the answer's in there."

"How so?" Mac asked.

"We're assuming the killer's paying close attention to media coverage of the case in order to get a line on how the investigation of the murder is going, right? That's why you planted a story on the unsuspecting reporters. Which, by the way, I'm peeved about because it's highly unethical. So, maybe there's something in the story quoting you that was a give-away to the killer."

Mac stroked his beard, possibly trying to decide whether he could buy that or not. Then he attacked the stack of papers with a will, muttering as he went.

First, he pawed through the papers at the top of the stack until he found Thursday's piece with the planted story. "I told Maggie very little. Yes, very little indeed. Except that—Could it be? Could it *possibly* be?"

Next, he picked up Maggie's account of the Calloway murder. And studied it intently. "What a fool I've been!" he exploded. "How could I have missed it?"

My wife, my sister, and I looked at each other and shrugged our shoulders. Sebastian McCabe no longer knew we were in the room.

Finally, he quickly scanned the profile of Grant Kingsley. When he put it down, the expression on his hirsute face was one I hadn't seen in a long time. It seemed to me a mixture of triumph and sorrow. Or at least, that's the way I remember it, knowing what I know now.

"What's the matter?" Kate said.

"I very much fear that I was right when I said the murderer was someone familiar on campus, but not so familiar as to go unnoticed without the camouflage afforded by the hoodie."

And then he told us who he meant.

"No," Lynda said. "I don't believe it. I won't believe it. You are bat-shit crazy, Mac."

"That may well be the case, dear friend. However, that does not mean that I am wrong. No matter what our hearts say, logic tells me otherwise."

Chapter Twenty-Seven
The Confession

"Maggie," Mac said, "I must make a confession."

"Don't tell me you did it!" She tried to make her tone light, but she didn't quite cut it.

Mac and I sat on one side of the conference table in the *Observer* offices on Monday morning, the first day of semester break, with Banfield and Gibbons on the other side. This time, they were supposed to keep quiet and let Mac run the show. They knew the bottom line of what was coming, but not all of it. Maggie sat at the head of the table, reporter's notebook in hand.

"My implication to you last Wednesday that I knew the identity of the murderer was a pretense, a ploy to lure the killer into launching yet another attack—this time on me."

That was as close as we would come to a confession from anybody that day.

"You used me." Maggie sounded hurt.

"I apologize. However, there was no attempted murder of Sebastian McCabe for the very good reason that the killer knew that I was not even close. I asked myself how that could be. Then I thought back to your responses in our conversations with you. When Jefferson artfully gave the impression that I knew the identity of the murderer, your first substantive question was not 'who is it?' but 'why are you calling me'? Surely that was an unusual question for a journalist to ask a regular source. The only way it made any sense, Maggie, is if you thought Jefferson might be calling you for a non-journalistic reason. I can hardly believe you would suspect blackmail, but perhaps you thought an old friend was calling to warn you."

"What are you saying, Mac?"

He ignored that.

"And then when you called me, you asked if the killer was 'anybody I know' and then 'what do you think I should do?' In context, these questions make the most sense if you were attempting to find out if I had identified you as the killer."

"Me, a killer?" Her voice rose in outrage, real or simulated. "I'm an old lady!" *With pink hair.*

"You are, however, a very angry old lady, Maggie. When I began reading through back issues of the *Observer* in my study yesterday, I realized that your account of Dr. Calloway's murder described the blow on the right side of her head, over her ear. You were not allowed inside the murder scene to see that, and Dr. Eppensteiner specifically asked that that detail not be shared with the media or the public."

"It was in the coroner's report." Maggie looked around the room, a sad appeal in her watery eyes.

"I'm sure it will be," Gibbons said, "but the report hasn't been released yet."

"Then I must have been confused. I get confused a lot lately. No doubt I was thinking about the Burch murder."

"But the coroner held back details there, too. They weren't published, not even in your paper."

"No, but Jeff told me off the record that pervert was hit on the right side of the head with a teaching award."

I avoided Gibbons' eyes, lest I be turned into stone or something. *You don't have to mention that to Arly Eppensteiner, do you, Jack?* I focused on Maggie.

"This is a pretty clever theory you're spinning, Mac," she said, "but I haven't heard anything that Marvin Slade would want to take to a jury."

"No doubt some unidentified fingerprints found at the murder scene will match yours," Mac offered.

She wasn't fazed. "Maybe so. I was in that office once, interviewing Dr. Calloway. St. Benignus has been my beat for more than twenty years, going back to when it was still a college. I've been all over the place."

Mac looked vindicated. "In fact, you are thoroughly accustomed to the campus, and yet not so familiar a sight as to be invisible." That was, of course, one of his criteria for the killer.

"BCI has the hoodie," Banfield told Maggie. "There's bound to be some DNA on it that we can match up to yours."

"Is that another ploy?"

"No," Gibbons said. "Don't you watch *CSI?*"

"Not often. But as a reporter, I should have thought to ask about tests on the hoodie. We'll see what turns up with that."

"Don't say anything else, Maggie," I advised. "Not until you get a lawyer. Hire Erica Slade, if you can."

Now I *was* an old friend warning her.

She smiled. "Thanks, Jeff. I've always liked you. You're okay, as flacks go. But I think we can chat a little bit before I call Erica. I may get a story out of this. So, Mac, do you have any idea why I would have killed Dr. Calloway?"

He nodded. "Motive is often where I begin to see daylight in a case. In this one, that was not so. Nevertheless, a motive does suggest itself as I reason backwards from your guilt. I venture to say that you blamed Dr. Calloway for the death of your great-niece, Mallory Lambert."

"Didn't she play for the Lady Dragons?" Banfield asked.

"She did until she was sidelined by an injury," I said. "She shattered her tibia and her fibula." I'd looked that up.

"Mallory had eleven operations," Maggie said in a dead voice. "Such a sweet girl. And funny. And giving—she volunteered reading to kids at St. Edward the Confessor grade school."

"The pain from the injury and all those operations must have been almost intolerable," Mac said in an empathetic tone. "As her team's physician, Helen Calloway prescribed Mallory oxycodone to deal with that. I confirmed this with her parents. Mallory became an addict and died of an overdose, for which you blamed Dr. Calloway. I myself experienced the doctor's lack of caution in prescribing that remedy. She offered to do so for me, a stranger although a colleague of sorts. That happened at the funeral home on the night of the Burch and Lambert visitations."

"I know. I heard her."

"Is that what set you off on your course of vengeance, spurred by the knowledge that Dr. Calloway had violated no law and could not be held accountable?"

"Some people would call what happened to her justice, not vengeance." *Justice is not a DIY project.* Marvin Slade had said that. "But, I'm sorry, Mac—go on. This is your story. Just how did I go about killing Dr. Calloway?"

"You must have called her and asked for an immediate interview," Mac said. "Perhaps you told her you were already on campus and pleaded the need to meet a deadline."

"For a story about what?"

"One can only conjecture. Opioids, perhaps? That would have been a nice irony."

She nodded. "Yes, I can see that. So, I show up at this interview wearing a hoodie?"

"That was an elementary precaution against being seen by someone who knew you. It would hide much of your face, draw scant attention, and be easy to discard—as it was. Incidentally, something else I realized in looking at that stack of *Observers* on Sunday was that you were on campus at the time Helen Calloway was killed. The murder happened right before your interview with Grant Kingsley." Mac looked at me. "In fact, Maggie was still in his office not so far away from the Athletics Building when word of the second murder reached you, Jefferson."

I remembered how she had looked when she arrived for the interview, almost breathless and distracted.

"How could she be sure there wasn't anybody around Dr. Calloway to see her?" I asked. How could any killer? That had bothered me all along.

"She could not be sure, Jefferson. However, the academic calendar and the time of day made an empty Athletics Building likely. If there had been someone unexpectedly on the scene, she could have postponed her plan for another day. In the event, that was not necessary. Dr. Calloway was alone. Did you confront her with your grievance, Maggie? I doubt it. More likely, you picked up the trophy and struck her unawares from behind, exactly as Warren Burch was attacked."

"Why did I kill Burch?" Maggie asked.

"Good question," Banfield said. "Why did you?"

Maggie shook her pink-haired head. "I had no reason to kill him."

"You made it clear in your hopelessly unbalanced news stories about him that you regarded the man as a sleaze," I pointed out.

"Guilty on that one. But if I killed every sleaze in this town, we'd have to replace most of City Council. I felt a lot of sympathy for those girls Burch humiliated, but I did something about it. I reported the facts that you people—yes, you, Jeff—wanted swept under the rug. That's how I took care of the old horndog. I repeat, I had no reason to kill him."

Maggie was giving Mac quite a run for his money, with a few lumps on the side to me. And who knew that she knew such words?

"Well, the same person killed both," Gibbons asserted.

"Exactly!" Maggie said. She seemed to be enjoying herself! "I think that puts you folks in a pickle. I was with

Mallory's family the night Burch met his Maker. She died earlier that day. And what about the surveillance video of Mackie Hall that I don't show up on?"

"How did you know the murderer didn't show up on the surveillance video?" Gibbons asked. *Don't look at me!* He looked at me.

"I didn't say the killer didn't. I said I didn't. I wasn't there."

"For now, I think one murder is enough to hold you," Gibbons said. "Margaret Barton, you are under arrest. You have the right to remain silent and to not answer . . ."

When he finished, Maggie pulled a set of keys out of her purse and pressed them on me. "Will you please have Lynda feed my cats for me? I may not be home for a while."

"I feel sorry for Maggie," I told Mac in the car, "and you know Lynda is devastated. I must admit, though, I'm glad for my own selfish reasons that the killer wasn't a member of the St. Benignus community."

"And yet," Mac muttered, "perhaps I have been too hasty in the matter of the second murder."

"Eh? What? You're not worried about Maggie's alibi and you being unable to explain how she reached Burch without showing on the cameras, are you?"

He waved that away like the non-existent smoke coming from his unlit cigar. "Not at all, old boy. Motive is what concerns me. As Maggie pointed out, she had no compelling reason that we know of to kill Warren Burch."

Chapter Twenty-Eight
Too Many Clues

Semester break went on for another month, until January 14, but there was no break in the Burch-Calloway murders.

Despite the usual chaos at Chez Cody on Tuesday morning, it seemed unearthly quiet at the breakfast table. That's because Lynda's normally vigorous voice was stilled by the *Observer*'s banner headline, **VETERAN REPORTER CHARGED WITH MURDER**. Tall Rawls, a good egg, wrote the story with all the professionalism I expected: "Margaret Barton, 76, long-time reporter for the *Erin Observer & News-Ledger*, was charged Monday . . ." Frank Woodford, as editor, wrote a signed editorial promising fair coverage of the case. Presumably he wasn't on the golf course because of the snow that promised a white Christmas.

Lynda put down the paper with a sigh. "Well, now we know why Maggie was so dogged about covering the Calloway murder—she wanted to find out if Mac was getting close to her. Why the hell did she have to go and kill the doctor? Maybe she didn't. Are you sure she did?"

"Pretty sure. When has Mac ever taken a wrong idea about a case this far?"

It didn't help Lynda's peace of mind a bit that Mac credited her for saying—rightly—that the solution to the murders lurked in the stack of newspapers in his man cave.

In a major blow to Maggie's defense, Erica Slade declined to represent her because of her, Erica's, personal relationship to the Burch case. But Evan Farleigh, with almost no experience in criminal law, offered to take her on. Maggie agreed, which I figured was tantamount to throwing in the towel. Ironically, Marvin then announced that he only planned to go to trial on the Calloway murder in view of Maggie's age and to spare Burch's victim-survivors from having to testify. He reserved the right to change his mind in the unlikely event that he didn't win a conviction in the Calloway case.

Meanwhile, life went on.

Mac finished *Quicker Than the Eye*, his latest Damon Devlin mystery.

Lynda was hard at work on the second draft of *her* novel, *Bluegrass,* sandwiched in between nursing the twins, playing with Donata, and last-minute Christmas shopping.

Popcorn and I proof-read the alumni magazine with Lynda's cover-story feature on Father Joe and sent it to the printer.

Gibbons showed up on campus, seen in the company of Banfield around lunch time, twice in the days immediately after Maggie's arrest. What a dedicated cop!

The search committee looking for a new president set a meeting schedule, but other than that the process was dead in the water until after the first of the year. Meanwhile, GK settled into the president's chair. In fact, he was so settled in that I wondered whether he would ever leave it. Father Joe spent an hour or two a day in his small office on the same floor, and his temporary successor occasionally dropped by for a dose of wisdom.

When Triple M, Kate, and a few more of Lynda's gal pals invaded our happy home the Thursday before Christmas, I fled to Mac's. In so doing, I managed to escape the predictable barrage of cute comments about the lack of kid-pickable ornaments on the tree (i.e., any below four feet from the floor). I found my brother-in-law in the man cave, sitting at his desk, and all-but-ignoring the roaring fire.

"What are you doing?" I asked.

"Trying to ferret out the real killer of Warren Burch."

"Still worrying that bone, are you?"

"I cannot let it alone. Or, rather, it will not let me alone." He looked at the mess on his desktop and sighed. "Both victims were struck from behind, to the right, and with a teaching award in one case and an athletic trophy in the other—clearly parallels. Obvious inference: two murders, one murderer. However, the second murder was so like the first that it was immediately suspect in my mind. After all, 'There is nothing more deceptive than an obvious fact.' To use your own felicitous phrase, Jefferson, there were too many clues. I erred in pushing that out of my mind.

"And at the same time, there is the puzzle of the virtually locked room in the circumstance of Professor Burch's murder which was not repeated in the case of Dr. Calloway. Why?"

My head was starting to hurt.

"You solved two murders. Why can't you just take your bows and move on? You're overthinking this. The explanation for the oh-so-obvious similarities is simple: Maggie must have been trying to make sure she got credit for both murders—some weird, psycho killer thing."

"And yet, she denies both."

"Don't be so logical. The old gal must be unhinged. If I were Farleigh, I'd get her to plead insanity."

"Have you forgotten that Gibbons confirmed her alibi for the Burch murder with Brian Lambert, her nephew?"

"Not exactly a disinterested party. I'm sure he loves his aunt. Heck, I love her myself and we're not even related."

"Also, Warren Burch was killed late in the evening. You will recall that at Hawes & Holder, after she left her great-niece's visitation, Maggie told us she no longer drives at night."

That stopped me for about ten seconds.

"Maybe she just said that to give herself a backup alibi!"

"And then not mention it when she was confronted? That hardly seems likely, old boy."

I was fast getting lost in the swamp without a paddle. Or something like that.

"What do you think happened?"

"I believe that Maggie, having determined to dispatch Dr. Calloway, decided to do so in such a way that the murderer of Warren Burch would be blamed. Perhaps she was even inspired in her homicidal intent by the murder of Professor Burch. Presumably, she had no fear of being successfully prosecuted for both because of her alibi and her lack of motive in the case of Burch. Although it did not work out in practice, she had every reason to believe that being exculpated in the first murder would lead to the same result in the second.

"Having thought all this out, she uniquely had the information necessary to stage a 'copycat' murder. Only Dr. Calloway's killer knew where and with what she was struck. For Maggie to include that information in her story was a serious misstep that helped lead to her undoing. However, thanks to your indiscretion, Professor Burch's killer is not the only one who knew details unknown to the public—Maggie also knew. You told her off the record, in my presence."

Rub it in, why don't you.

"Okay, but if Maggie didn't kill Burch, then who did?"

That was supposed to be a rhetorical question, but Mac didn't take it that way.

"I have an answer to that, Jefferson. I have had it for several days. The prosecutor has the same answer—and that is the real reason he is not prosecuting Maggie for the Burch murder. Yet all my instincts rebel at that solution. There must be a flaw in my thinking somewhere, and a different answer."

Mac stared moodily at his desk. "That is what I was pondering when you entered. Perhaps we need to revisit our earlier work."

He fished through the papers on his desk and picked up a familiar document, the one headed:

THE THREE STUDENTS
A Chronology

He glanced at it, set it aside, then grabbed it again. "By thunder, there it is! The three students!"

"But we already exculpated them!" That sounded dirty, but if Mac could use the word, so could I. "The timetable was a dead end."

"Indeed, it was, old boy, in the sense that you mean it. The only timetable that really matters is examination week. I believe I know why Warren Burch was killed and how his killer eluded the video surveillance. A look at the video should confirm my conjecture. I do not yet know the killer's identity, but I am confident that it is not beyond reach. Regardless, we need to speak to the Slades on neutral territory. Mo's Mysteries & Marvels should do nicely."

"Slades plural? All three of them?"

"Just the parents should suffice."

Chapter Twenty-Nine
Mysteries & Marvels

Friday, December 21, the last day the Office of Communications was open before Christmas, Popcorn and I had our own little party late in the afternoon. She brought the cookies and I supplied the eggnog. Snow still covered the ground, setting the mood nicely. I put on a CD of Old Blue Eyes singing Christmas songs and opened the bottle of eggnog—bourbon, rum, and brandy already included. We consumed the seasonal beverage in moderation and shared it with Mac and Oscar when they stopped by. Oscar wore his Santa Claus hat.

When the CD ended, we did our own singing. By the time we finished "O Come, All Ye Faithful," GK, Saylor-Mackie, and two or three other denizens of the fourth and fifth floors had crowded into the office. Then it was on to "Silent Night." At the end, surprisingly, Oscar burst into a solo of the same in German:

Stille Nacht, heilige Nacht,

Then Mac joined in with:

Alles schläft, einsam wacht
Nur das traute hochheilige Paar.
Holder Knab' im lockigten Haar,
Schlaf in himmlischer Ruh!
Schlaf in himmlischer Ruh!

When they finished, we all clapped and GK shooed us out of the Gamble Building to begin our Christmas weekend a couple of hours early. In some ways, it was the best party ever. I felt all warm and Christmasy. I wanted to go home to Lynda and the kids and light a fire (or two, if you catch my drift). But that would have to wait.

Mo's Mysteries & Marvels bookstore, purveying both mystery and science fiction/fantasy books from a former firehouse on Water Street, also closed early that day. But not for Mac. As the supposedly silent partner, he has full access whenever he wants. He opened it for Marvin and Erica Slade that afternoon, their earliest convenience.

We sat in a side room at a big round table used for meetings of the Poisoned Pens mystery writers' group and the science fiction book club to which Triple M belongs. Even round tables have sides, of a sort. Mac and I sat facing the Slades. Mac sat his walking stick on an empty chair.

Erica wore a red V-neck knit dress, red heels, and red earrings shaped like Christmas lights. Marvin wore a red face.

"As I told you on the phone, I'm here against my better judgement," he huffed. "I'm deeply concerned that discussing a case which I may take to court in the future is highly problematical."

"Oh, stuff it, Marvin," Erica directed. "You couldn't stay away because you're as curious as I am."

He shifted his glare from Mac to his ex-wife. "Well, if you were going to be here, I wasn't going to not be here."

Double negatives confuse me, Marv.

Mac harrumphed. "At any rate, I am pleased you are both here because I have something to say for the benefit of both of you. Let me begin with a fact which I believe that at least you, Mr. Slade, are aware of: Maggie Barton killed Dr. Helen Calloway, but she did not kill Warren Burch."

Erica's violet eyes opened wider, but that was the only tell that she was surprised, and I only saw that because I was looking for it. Marvin, on the other hand, completely overplayed the pretense of surprise:

"What the hell are you talking about?"

He knew the answer to his own question, so Mac addressed Erica. "From almost the moment that Dr. Calloway's body was found, it seemed evident that she was killed by whomever murdered her St. Benignus colleague. There were many indications of that—too many clues, in fact."

Mac went on, laying it out as he had for me the day before in his study, but this time without my incisive interventions.

"I know I'm going to hate myself for asking this," Erica said, "but if Maggie didn't kill Burch, who did?"

Marvin stood up. "I'm not sure I should hear this."

"You should," Mac said. "On that you have my word."

"Hear him out," Erica said.

"Are you sure?"

"The man has a better track record than you do, Marvin."

"That's what worries me." He sat down again, but he looked worried.

"When I became morally certain that Maggie's immortal soul is burdened with the guilt of only one murder, I revisited the killing of Warren Burch. And I realized that we had such a plentitude of obvious suspects that I had failed to ask myself a question that has often helped me in the past: What changed with Professor Burch's absence from the scene?"

"A big PR problem for you went away," Marvin tossed off in my direction.

"Good try," I told him.

Mac ignored the byplay.

"As you yourself noted in our meeting in your office, Ms. Slade, the Burch murder meant that he would never be charged with sexual imposition if a certain young lady changed her mind and decided to come forward. Hence, he would never face a trial. Hence, your daughter would not have to appear as a witness as you once did in a traumatic situation that bothers you to this day."

That kind of sucked the air out of the room for a while.

"Well," Erica said finally, "that's all true." She crossed her legs. I tore the Cody eyes away from her lovely ankles. "And if you're going where I think you're going, this is a very interesting theory you have."

Mac nodded. "That would be one adjective for it. However, it was not my theory alone. You, Mr. Slade, also realized that your former wife and the mother of your daughter had a solid motive for killing Warren Burch—to protect the young woman you both love."

"That's ridiculous!"

Not only was that a terrible line—*don't try to get a job in Hollywood writing dialogue, Marv*—he delivered it so poorly as to make it clear that Mac had hit a bullseye.

Erica stared—not at Mac, but at Marvin.

"That is why you announced that you would recuse yourself from prosecuting Warren Burch's killer, Mr. Slade," Mac went on. "That is why, later, you announced that your office will prosecute Maggie for only one murder. You even told Jefferson and me, confidentially, that you were thinking of remarrying your former wife. Perhaps there was more than one reason for that intention, the human heart being the great mystery that it is, but I note that once remarried you could not be forced to testify against your wife."

"Is this true, Marvin?" Erica snapped. "It's true, isn't it?"

He looked miserable. "Can I take the fifth?"

"You complete, total, utter *asshole!*" She grabbed him and kissed him hard on the mouth. He did not resist.

Mac cleared his throat, which sounded like the rumble of a coal-fired locomotive. "Mr. Slade, as a citizen I find your actions reprehensible in a prosecuting attorney. As a husband and father, I deeply sympathize."

"Listen, asshole," Erica told her ex-husband. "What makes you think I would even *think* of remarrying you?" *I think you're sending mixed messages here, what with the kiss and all.*

Marvin dodged the question and instead defended himself. "I called you the night Burch died to try to work out something for Christmas as a family. You didn't answer. You always answer my calls, so you must have had a good reason. I didn't think your unavailability to me that particular night was a coincidence."

"Well, it was. I had my ringtone turned off because I was out on a date with a guy who turned out to be even more boring than you. By the time I saw you called, it was late and I figured you'd call me back if it was important."

"If I may resume," Mac said heavily. "I have shared with you the train of thought that I reached earlier this week. It was sound, logical, and totally unbelievable. For one thing, if Ms. Slade chose to engage in homicide, I could not credit that she would be so stealthy about it. That is not in her forceful nature. In addition, the idea that someone with no connection to St. Benignus University had showed up on campus late in the evening, evaded the security cameras, and committed murder, was simply not tenable."

"Then who?"

It would be satisfying to report that at that very moment a shop bell jingled to announce that someone had entered the store, despite the **CLOSED** sign, and that the someone was the killer. But it didn't happen quite that way.

"We are expecting visitors soon," Mac said in reply, after a glance at his Sherlock Holmes wristwatch. "Perhaps it would be best if I explained this just once after our company is complete." He pulled out a deck of cards, which he held out to Erica. "In the interim, pick a card, any card."

Chapter Thirty
Final Exam

Mac had barely finished the trick, pulling the King of Hearts out of his cigar, when the shop bell above the door announced the arrival of a caller.

He raised an eyebrow. "Our first guest is early. I suppose I should have expected that."

Looking hesitant, a slight young man with fair hair worn down to his collar made his way to the back of the store.

"Jason Danvers, I presume?" Mac said.

"Right. You must be Professor McCabe. You wanted to see me? Something about Professor Burch that you said I'd be interested in?"

"Who is this?" Marvin Slade demanded.

"I know that name from somewhere," Erica said. She doesn't miss much.

"Warren Burch's strongest and most persistent advocate in the twitterverse," I supplied.

"So, what's this all about?" Danvers persisted. "And who are these people?"

Mac introduced them by name and occupation, unnecessarily pointing to each in turn with his walking stick. "Before I explain the purpose of this meeting, I await the presence of two law enforcement officials."

Danvers's face made all kinds of maneuvers, starting from the moment he heard the words "county prosecutor" after Marvin's moniker. But he finally settled on a "confident young collegiate" façade.

"I can't hang around. I have a party to go to."

"Well, I have no authority to detain you, but perhaps I can entertain you." *No more magic tricks, please!* "Please sit down."

Danvers did so, warily, settling in about half-way between me and Erica.

"Here is a riddle," Mac continued. "When is a joke not a joke?"

"When it's taken seriously," Erica said quickly. I guess she wanted to beat Marvin to the punch, but he looked thoroughly confused. I couldn't blame him; I was confused, and I knew the end game.

"What the fudge?" Danvers didn't really say fudge. Mac ignored the outburst.

"Spot on!" he told Erica. "Jefferson here and a certain young lady"—he meant Zoe Slade—"at different times suggested in jest that one of Warren Burch's current students may have killed him because his tests were so difficult. For too long, I made the mistake of taking those comments in the spirit in which they were made.

"That changed when I looked at a certain document of my own creation in a new light. It was a timetable of Warren Burch's offenses, headed 'The Three Students.' My mind suddenly went to a Sherlock Holmes story of that name—'The Adventure of the Three Students,' to be precise."

"Sherlock Holmes," Slade muttered, not in a worshipful tone.

His ex cut him down with a look.

"Are you going to listen to this?" Danvers asked Slade. Mac resumed before the prosecutor could reply.

"The theme of that story is the theft of an examination paper, which set me to thinking. Professor Burch died on the cusp of examination week. Perhaps his murder, which by all appearances was unpremeditated, happened during the attempted theft of his upcoming final examination paper. Was there any confirmation for this?

There was, at least, an intriguing possibility. Officer Jackson testified that he heard the office photocopying machine the night of the murder. What better way to steal a paper without making it obvious than by photocopying it?"

"That's a little thin." Erica sounded like she was already planning a defense strategy.

"It gets fatter when you know that Warren Burch *could not have been the person that Officer Jackson heard operating the machine.* The reason is that he was not yet in the building. When Chief Decker described the video to Jefferson and me, he said it showed Professor Burch arriving, then later leaving and returning with Chinese takeout. He also said it showed Officer Jackson entering the building twice on his rounds. When I viewed the video earlier today, by Chief Decker's sufferance, I confirmed that Burch arrived *after* Officer Jackson entered the building the second time and heard the machine in operation.

"Of itself that is not determinative. However, it is indicative. So is the murder weapon—a teaching award, which implied a certain animus in that direction. I felt reasonably sure that I was sound in suspecting that Burch interrupted a student in the act of copying an examination paper for the purpose of achieving a better grade."

"Even if you're by some chance right," Slade said, not to be outdone by Ms. Slade in the skepticism department, "how could you narrow it down to a particular student? Burch must have had dozens."

"Not that many. He only taught two classes. Still, the identity of the killer only came to me late last night in my study after I sent Jefferson on his way. I got to that by first inventorying what is known or can be reasonably assumed about the killer. First, he or she is not a good student—why else have recourse to steal the examination paper? Second, this person's academic success must be extraordinarily important to him or her, or else why take such drastic measures as thievery in the night? Third, the thief must be familiar with the Professor's office, or else why even think that he or she could find the examination paper, copy it, and get away with it? Jefferson and I recently had another case, a small matter of robbery, in which it was similarly clear that the felon had inside information."

Santa Crook! No need to tell Marvin any more about that.

"When I put all this together, I immediately thought of an individual I myself had never met, although Jefferson had told me much about him. His parents were both highly successful in their careers, and so must have had high hopes for him. And yet, his grades were not of the best. Surely, they were disappointed with him, and perhaps made that clear."

"That's a lie!" Danvers snapped. The look in his eyes was almost feral.

"You assume that I refer to you, Mr. Danvers, and rightly so. It may interest you to learn that I spoke today with Professor Wendy Yazane, who administered the examination just as Warren Burch wrote it. She informed me that you did remarkably well, demonstrating a command of the material far beyond any you showed in previous tests.

"To the third point of my description of the killer, it is no great leap to posit that you were familiar with Professor Burch's office. As he was your advisor, you must have met with him there often. Undoubtedly you did not, however, know that he was occasionally in that office quite late. That is why you were taken unawares as you attempted to copy the examination paper. Only later did you pretend to know of his working habits."

Danvers said nothing.

"I saw those tweets about Burch supposedly being so hard-working, the late hours and all that," Erica said. "What's with the tweet storm? Why call attention to himself?"

"Almost certainly his original intention in defending his advisor so vigorously in the wake of Maggie's stories was to curry favor with a professor known to craft rigorous final examinations. Having thus created the persona of the admiring tweeter, he could scarcely remain silent about the murder. That would have been a strange silence."

Like the dog in the night-time! But please don't say that.

After all this, the best Danvers could manage was:

"Nobody saw the killer. He didn't even show up on the security video."

Mac nodded. "True enough—and a fact presumably known to the killer, but not to the public. It was not reported. The killer's apparent invisibility puzzled me so much that I put it to one side while I pursued other lines of thought. The solution came to me at the same time I realized that the original sin in this case was academic thievery. A clue to the *how* was buried in the sordid conduct of Professor Burch himself. My 'Three Students' chronology reminded me that one of his accusers testified that the dean—as he was then— asked her to stand on a chair and adjust an air vent in the ceiling so that he could look up her dress. This conduct was mentioned in the investigative report and in Maggie Burch's *Observer* story. The young woman told us the same thing. Warren Burch's new office as a professor, which is in the same building, also had an air vent. I noticed it myself when I was in the murder room."

So did I.

"An air vent meant an air duct, and this one was right above Professor Burch's desk. And there it was: The killer entered the murder room through an air duct, just like the notorious dormitory burglar Pierce Brooks[10]. He lowered himself to the desk and departed the same way. The Brooks case, which caused so much embarrassment to the campus police, was well covered in both the *Observer* and the *Spectator*.

---

[10] Jefferson mentions this individual in Chapter Five. Only later, during the trial of Jason Danvers, did I learn of a *New York Times* report on May 4, 2017 that a student at the University of Kentucky used an air duct to gain access to an instructor's office for the purpose of stealing a copy of an examination paper for a statistics class. As Sherlock Holmes said, "It's all been done before and will be again."—*S. McC.*

As a student, you could scarcely *not* know about it, Mr. Danvers. I presume you entered the duct at some other point, perhaps the men's rest room, toward the end of normal business hours and there awaited your opportunity. Thus, Officer Jackson never saw you."

Dust and dirt! I'd seen it on the papers scattered over Burch's desk, right beneath the air vent. It must have entered the room with Danvers.

"How would I even know where the duct work ran so that I could get into it and into Burch's office?"

"The schematic plans are a matter of public record with the Erin Department of Buildings and Inspections. As the son of a successful architect, you would either know that or could quickly learn it with a casual question to your father.

"Being of small stature, you would not find the air duct such a tight squeeze—although I imagine the wait was nevertheless a long and unpleasant one. Perhaps you were about to lower yourself into the room after the cleaning crew left, only to hear Professor Burch arrive. When he finally departed hours later, you assumed that his work was done. That turned out to be a fatal mistake—fatal for Warren Burch when he unpredictably brought his takeout dinner back to the office. No doubt you acted on impulse when you saw disaster looming before you. And yet, I rather think the use of a teaching award to end that threat was no fluke. You must have spent a very long night in that vent before exiting the next morning when the coast was clear, presumably at the point where you entered."

Marvin thought a minute. "Why didn't he just run out of the front door afterwards?"

"Mr. Danvers?" Taking his sullen look for a "no comment," Mac replied: "Most likely he was aware of the video surveillance. It was installed last year with some fanfare. In addition, he would have heard Officer Jackson conversing with Burch earlier in the evening and may have feared that he, too, would return."

Danvers squeezed his hands into fists. "You tell a nice story. Fiction is your wheelhouse, McCabe, and you should stick to it. I didn't hear any proof."

My turn.

"Hadley Reams knew about Burch's murder before anybody in the professional media," I said. "He wouldn't tell me how, pleading 'sources.' But you were in his office that morning. I imagine you were trying to cozy up to him so that you could get close to the case. That seems like your style."

Erica Slade shook her head—a bit sadly, I thought. "Sorry, Jeff, but that's hardly proof."

Mac's turn.

"You are a young man who causes himself a lot of trouble by his failure to take pains, Mr. Danvers. If some of the unidentified fingerprints on the copying machine turn out to be yours, that is easily explained by Professor Burch's role as your adviser. He may have granted you permission to use the machine, or even asked you to do so on his behalf. I concede that. However, your prints on the inside of the air duct would be harder to explain. Did you take the pains to wipe them off? Ah, I thought not."

The panic in his face reached his feet and Danvers bolted. Where he thought he could go, I have no idea, but he stood up and started to move.

Erica moved faster. Not having her famous boxing gloves handy, she picked Mac's walking stick off the chair and inserted it between Danvers' moving legs. Danvers went down fast and not quietly. He displayed an impressive vocabulary of words that used to be unprintable. And he was still yelling when the shop bell jingled, announcing the arrival of Aurelia Banfield and L. Jack Gibbons.

"I guess we're a little late," Banfield said.

"Not too late to make an arrest," Marvin Slade informed her. "And I don't care which one of you does it."

Chapter Thirty-One
Jailhouse Christmas

I don't know about you, but it's not every Christmas that Lynda and I face the decision of when to go to church and when to go to jail—for a visit. We finally decided to drag three sleeping kids off to midnight Mass and see Maggie in the morning. Late morning.

"How's the food?" I asked the old gal, just to get the conversational ball rolling.

"Food? Is that what you call it?" She didn't seem to have lost any weight. In fact, she looked just the same except that her white roots were showing beneath the pink. "How are my Binkie and Bunkie?"

Those damned cats!

"They're fine. "We visit them several times a day. Sometimes we even take them home with us. They love the kids. You should be worrying about yourself, Maggie, not them."

"Don't be silly. I'm in good hands, defense-wise. Erica offered to take my case pro bono, so I fired Farleigh and let her at it."

Maggie's confidence was not misplaced. After just a few weeks on the job, Erica learned—to the shock of even Sebastian McCabe—that Dr. Calloway hadn't just been careless in writing prescriptions. She'd also been trafficking on a medium-sized scale in oxycodone. Apparently, she tried to bail out her husband's failing dog training business by making money on the side.

Mac thinks that explains why Dr. Calloway agreed to meet Maggie that day at the Athletics Building: Maggie must have called and said she wanted to talk to her about prescription opioids. The good doctor wrongly assumed that Maggie had somehow learned about her sideline and was selling her silence. "That is the merest speculation, of course," Mac cautioned. I would say "the jury is still out on that," but the jury hasn't even been impaneled yet.

Dr. Calloway's crime didn't come close to justifying murder, but it will most likely whip up sympathy for Maggie with the twelve people who counted.

Jason Danvers is another matter. His parents managed to hire the second most-famous defense attorney in the country, John Henry Clayton of Chicago, but I still think it's a lost cause. He hasn't been tweeting lately, probably on advice of counsel.

Recently I heard that Catherine Burch and Roger Calloway joined the same grief-support group and are now "keeping company." There's an irony in there somewhere.

All of this was still in the future on Christmas Day at what I like to call "Oscar's B&B," the city jail.

"Now that I'm an inmate, Oscar treats me better than he did when I was a reporter," Maggie said. "I'm not kidding about that."

"I didn't think you were," Lynda assured her.

We talked for another half-hour or so, carefully avoiding any possibility that she could say something incriminating. I didn't think the jail was bugged, but Oscar surprises me sometimes. Then we were off to Chez Cody, more than a little sadly, to celebrate Christmas and Donata's birthday with Clan McCabe.

Lynda whipped up an Italian Christmas dinner, with braciola for the entrée and cannoli for dessert. *Mamma mia!*

In the evening we sat around the kid-proof family room, comfortably stuffed, surveying the wreckage of toys opened with great joy and quickly discarded for the next one. And that was just the adults.

"It's funny," I mused. "Gibbons had the right answer to the wrong case."

"How so, old boy?" Mac barely opened his eyes.

"Last year, in that business of the opera murders, he theorized that the killer was a copycat. Right answer, wrong case."

He chuckled. "Well, let us hope that the worthy Gibbons does not make a habit of that."

"What do you mean?" Kate asked.

"He suspected Grant Kingsley of killing Warren Burch. I should certainly hate for that to be the solution to the next murder that comes our way!"

Yes, there would be another murder case for McCabe & Cody. But that, of course, is another story.

A Few Words of Thanks

This is the ninth novel, and tenth book, in the chronicles of Sebastian McCabe and Jeff Cody. Jeff originally expected that each book would be subtitled "A Sebastian McCabe Mystery," but was forced to add his own name to the series in response to popular demand.

An amazing eight years after *No Police Like Holmes* first saw the light of day, Jeff is "the same blithe boy as ever," as Holmes said of Watson in "His Last Bow." Although matured a bit by marriage and fatherhood—well, no, he isn't. And he plans to continue writing these adventures for a long time to come.

But Jeff doesn't do that alone. So, thanks to:

Ann Brauer Andriacco, who I have sometimes referred to as my co-conspirator;

Gary Miller, a faithful reader who is now a beta reader as the newest member of Team Cody;

Kieran McMullen, who once more provided invaluable feedback on matters homicidal and details of police procedure;

Jeff Suess, for proofreading and final preparation of the manuscript; and

Steve Winter, yet again, for giving the manuscript the incredible benefit of his engineering eye.

Publisher Steve Emecz and cover illustrator Brian Belanger are the easiest collaborators any writer was ever so lucky to have. MX Publishing is a social enterprise venture that is both enterprising and venturesome.

About the Author

Dan Andriacco has been reading mysteries since he discovered Sherlock Holmes at the age of nine, and writing them almost as long.

The first nine books in his popular Sebastian McCabe–Jeff Cody series are *No Police Like Holmes*, *Holmes Sweet Holmes*, *The 1895 Murder*, *The Disappearance of Mr. James Phillimore*, *Rogues Gallery* (shorter stories), *Bookmarked for Murder*, *Erin Go Bloody*, *Queen City Corpse*, and *Death Masque*. He is also the co-author, with Kieran McMullen, of *The Amateur Executioner*, *The Poisoned Penman*, and *The Egyptian Curse* mysteries solved by Enoch Hale with Sherlock Holmes.

Also the author of *Baker Street Beat: An Eclectic Collection of Sherlockian Scribblings*, Dan is the leader of the Tankerville Club of Cincinnati and a member the Illustrious Clients of Indianapolis, the Agra Treasurers of Dayton, Watson's Tin Box of Ellicott City, MD, and the Vatican Cameos—all scion societies of the Baker Street Irregulars. Follow Dan's long-running blog at www.danandriacco.com, his tweets at *@DanAndriacco*, and his Facebook Fan Page, Dan Andriacco Mysteries.

Dr. Dan and his co-conspirator, Ann Brauer Andriacco, have three grown children and six grandchildren. They live in Cincinnati, Ohio, USA, about forty miles downriver from Erin.

Praise for the McCabe–Cody mysteries

"Again, Andriacco displays an encyclopedic memory for his enormous roster of clever and colorful characters. There is never a lull in his writing, and he propels his story to a surprising conclusion for this reader. *Death Masque* is another witty and lively novel by Andriacco."
　　— Felicia Carparelli

"Dan Andriacco's *Queen City Corpse* is the latest in his series about Jeff Cody and Sebastian McCabe, who are in Cincinnati for a mystery convention and encounter mystery and murder, and a surprising solution; it's a lively story."
　　—Peter Blau in *Scuttlebutt from the Spermaceti Press*

"This *(Queen City Corpse)* is the seventh novel in a deliciously literate, witty series, with ingenious plots and engaging characters. Highly recommended!"
　　—*Sherlock Holmes Society of London*

"This (*Erin Go Bloody*) is Dan Andriacco's best book to date! I feel I could actually walk around downtown Erin, Ohio and not get lost. The characters are charming and believable. These are always entertaining reads!"
—Retired Sheriff Kenneth Ramsey, Sr.

"The ingenious twist at the end is an example of Andriacco's masterful ability to pen a page-turner. *Bookmarked for Murder* is a must-read for anyone who loves a classic who-done-it."
—Mystery writer Kathleen Kaska

"You're in the hands of a master of mystery plotting here. *Rogues Gallery* is a delightful read, hard to put down, and highly recommended. And did I say fun?"
—Screenwriter and novelist Bonnie MacBird

(*The Disappearance of Mr. James Phillimore*) "is a fun read in a series that keeps getting better with each new tale."
—Philip K. Jones

"*The* 1895 *Murder* is the most smoothly-plotted and written Cody/McCabe mystery yet. Mr. Andriacco plays fair with the reader, but his clues are deftly hidden, much as Sebastian McCabe hides the secrets to his magic tricks under an entertaining run of palaver."
—*The Well-Read Sherlockian*

"I loved Dan Andriacco's first novel about Sebastian McCabe and Jeff Cody, and I'm delighted to recommend (*Holmes Sweet Holmes*), which has a curiously topical touch."
—Roger Johnson, *Sherlock Holmes Society of London*

"*No Police Like Holmes* is a chocolate bar of a novel—delicious, addictive, and leaves a craving for more."
—*Girl Meets Sherlock*

Also from MX Publishing

Visit www.mxpublishing.com for dozens of other Sherlock Holmes novels, novellas, short story collections, Conan Doyle biographies, Holmes travel books, and more.

MX Publishing is the award-winning, world's largest independent Sherlock Holmes Book publishers with over 150 new authors and 500 new Sherlock Holmes stories in print.

On Facebook:
https://www.facebook.com/BooksSherlockHolmes/

On Twitter
https://twitter.com/mxpublishing

On Instagram
https://www.instagram.com/mxpublishing/